I0531541

Sky was human once. Now he's part demon, and he can't stop himself from catching fire every time he feels strongly about something. Any emotion will do—fear, shock, arousal. Being freed from the lab he'd spent almost a year in would be a good thing if he could control his new ability, but as it is, he risks setting the warehouse and the council assassins on fire, including his mate.

Ulric can't say he's happy about his mate's ability to control fire, but that's mostly because Sky can't control it right now. Even though Sky pushes Ulric away, he has help and people who can teach him what to do. The problem is that when it comes to Ulric, Sky doesn't seem to be able to keep his emotions in check, and that might mean they can never be together.

Ulric is ready to do everything he can to help Sky, even if it means getting burned here and there. Sky doesn't share that opinion, though, and he knows he has to learn control—or let Ulric go.

The unauthorized reproduction or distribution of this copyrighted work is illegal. Criminal copyright infringement, including infringement without monetary gain, is investigated by the FBI and is punishable by up to 5 years in federal prison and a fine of $250,000.

This book is a work of fiction. Names, characters, places, and incidents either are products of the author's imagination or are used fictitiously. Any resemblance to actual events or locales or persons, living or dead, is entirely coincidental.

Ulric
Copyright © 2019 Catherine Lievens
ISBN: 978-1-4874-2683-5
Cover art by Angela Waters

All rights reserved. Except for use in any review, the reproduction or utilization of this work in whole or in part in any form by any electronic, mechanical or other means, now known or hereafter invented, is forbidden without the written permission of the publisher.

Published by eXtasy Books Inc or
Devine Destinies, an imprint of eXtasy Books Inc

Look for us online at:
www.eXtasybooks.com or www.devinedestinies.com

ULRIC
COUNCIL ASSASSINS BOOK 8

BY

CATHERINE LIEVENS

CHAPTER ONE

Everything was the same. Everything was always the same. Sky knew the four walls of his cell by heart. He'd spent so much time staring at them that he could find specific cracks and stains. He didn't most of the time, but it wasn't like he had anything else to do. He'd rather be staring at walls than having the scientists poke and prod him until he did what they wanted. Things were always better when he was left alone in the cell—for everyone, including those damn scientists.

Sky leaned closer to the wall his bed was pushed against. He wrapped his arms around his knees and watched the door. He knew they'd come soon. It was time.

They never gave him a more than a few days between one experiment or the other. Even after he'd killed that guard, they've never stopped. He'd been horrified by that death, but they'd been over the moon over it. They wanted him to learn how to kill, to gain control.

He didn't.

Learning control would mean he'd have to leave. He didn't want that, either. He wasn't going anywhere, and that was for the best. One man had died, and that was more than enough for Sky. He wouldn't put anyone else in danger.

He probably could have found a way out of the lab. With the power the scientists had given him, there was little he couldn't do. Hell, he could burn down the building while sitting on his bed, and once everything was gone, he could walk out of the ruins. It would be easy. He only had to get angry or

1

scared, or to feel any other strong emotion. So far, he hadn't been able to stop himself from catching fire when he *felt*. That was why he was relieved when the scientists gave him pills to calm down or to sleep, but they hadn't done that in too long. They *needed* him to catch fire. He wouldn't learn control otherwise.

He didn't want to learn, though. He knew he should. It would be the best way to make sure no one else got hurt. But it would also give the scientists what they wanted. They were trying to turn Sky into a weapon and control him, but they needed him to be able to catch fire on command. He didn't know what would happen to him if he succeeded, but he could imagine it too easily.

Everyone in the lab was a weapon. That was the point of the lab. Sky had seen people coming in and going out. Some of them had been dead, and his heart hurt for them, even though he'd never talked to any of them. But some of them had been alive, and they'd obeyed the scientists and soldiers who'd come to pick them up. They've given up their freedom to get out of the lab, and Sky wasn't going to do that.

He would have given anything to be free a few months ago. He'd been in the lab for what felt like years, and maybe he had. He had no way to know how many days had passed. He didn't even know when it was night or day. There were no windows in the cell, or anywhere else in the lab. The only way for him to count the days that passed were the meals, but he couldn't trust that, either. Some of the guards liked starving Sky and the other prisoners. They shouldn't, because it could hinder the scientists' work, but they didn't care, and as long as the scientists didn't find out, they'd be fine. It wasn't like the scientists were going to believe or even listen to the prisoners.

And they were nothing more than that, nothing more than experiments.

Sky had been human once. He wasn't sure why they'd chosen him, of all people. He'd been human, nothing out of the ordinary. But now he was special. He hated it, but he knew he couldn't change it, not anymore. The scientists had gotten rid of his humanity and replaced it with an inferno of fire.

Sky had no idea how to deal with it.

At least the shifters knew how to handle having another side. He didn't. That was probably one of the reasons he had such a hard time controlling the fire. That, and his emotions were always high when scientists were poking at him.

They hadn't lately. It was a relief, because they usually wanted Sky to hurt people. They thought the only way for him to learn control was to use his power. That was exactly what he was trying to avoid. They wanted him to set people on fire.

He wanted to set himself on fire and die. He'd tried the first few days after he'd realized what he had become, but he hadn't succeeded. He *was* fire now, and the ability to die by fire was gone from him. He should be relieved, but he wasn't. It would have been the best and fastest way for him to be free. Instead, he was stuck here, in a fireproof room, at the mercy of the people who wanted him to become a killer.

He'd rather starve himself than do that.

Leaving the lab would mean killing people, and it was the biggest reason he hadn't. The scientists and the guards were always careful when they moved him from his cell, but it would be so easy to catch fire in the hallway. But what would Sky do once he was out? Even if he considered those necessary deaths, they were the only ones who deserved to die. What about the people out there? Sky could set them on fire with just a thought, an emotion, and he wouldn't do that. He was dangerous, and he belonged in the cell.

He just wished the scientists weren't still experimenting on him.

It was better than before. Now they had what they'd been searching for, which was that he could catch fire and never burn himself. They needed him to learn control so that he could set people and things on fire on purpose, following orders, but Sky had made sure to be uncooperative every time they attempted to teach him. He *wanted* to learn control, but not like this, not if meant becoming a killer. He wanted to leave the lab, but not at this price.

He didn't want anyone to have a say in what he could do. He didn't want anyone to give him orders. He didn't want anyone to make a killer out of him, especially after he'd already killed someone. He'd rather stay in this cell forever, even with the experiments still happening.

He jerked when he heard a noise outside in the hallway. People in the hallway were never a good thing, because it meant that Sky or one of the other people locked in the cells were about to be taken away. Some of them came back, but not all of them did. Some of them were never the same when they did. *None* of them wanted to go through whatever the scientists had planned for them.

Sky pressed his back against the wall and stared at the door. He held his breath until the guards stopped in front of the cell. They were there for him. He wasn't surprised. The scientists never listened when he said he didn't want to become a killer. No one did. It was like he wasn't even speaking. No one cared what he wanted. To them, he was nothing more than an experiment, a weapon, and they needed him to behave that way. When he didn't, bad things happened.

The door opened, squeaking. Two guards wearing fireproof suits stepped in. Sky didn't recognize them, not with the masks on, but who they were didn't matter. All the guards did with the scientists ordered them to do. None of them cared what happened to the people they dragged from their cells. None of them cared if people, human beings, were being turned into weapons against their will, were tortured until they did what they were told.

Their job was to follow orders, and that was what they did, without pity for anyone and without thinking twice about it.

Still, Sky didn't make it easy for them. It wasn't even on purpose. His hands caught fire, then the rest of him. He always did that when he was taken away because he was afraid. Eventually, he'd burn through the suits, but of course, the guards knew that. They always made sure to drag him out of the cell and to the lab as fast as they could.

He was dangerous. They knew it. They'd made him so. That was why they kept him there, why they wanted him to learn control.

They wanted to send him out into the world to kill people they wanted to get rid of.

He wouldn't do it, whatever happened to him, whatever they did.

Ulric itched to do something. He'd had enough of sitting at home waiting for the council to decide the time had arrived. He wanted to do something, anything, to help. The thought of people being prisoners, being hurt every day while they waited, made him want to punch the wall.

"When are we leaving?" he asked.

Win glared at him. "As soon as we get the go-ahead from the council, like I just told you."

"The council is slow. We need to move right now. The lab is in the city. We can go in, kill the bad guys, and take the good guys home."

"Or we can wait for the council to tell us it's time for us to go."

Ulric scowled. He knew Win had to obey the council. They all did. Their little group existed only thanks to the council.

They'd all be locked up or something similar if the council hadn't reached out to them. That didn't mean the council knew what they were doing.

Ulric understood waiting until they were sure of what was happening. He understood being careful. He understood wanting to do things the right way. He *wanted* to do things the right way, but not when other people were in danger. In that case, he didn't care about the right thing. He wanted to help, to get those people out of the lab, right now.

The council couldn't understand what it was like to be in there. Ulric and his friends did, though. They'd been through it themselves. They knew exactly how it felt to be considered nothing more than an experiment, an animal. They knew how it felt to be afraid of every single noise, of every time the door opened. And even once they were released, the fear hadn't ended.

There was the fear of being taken again. The fear of being different, of not knowing what to do now. The fear of hurting people because he didn't know how to control what he had become.

The people in the lab wouldn't be able to start healing until they were out of there. That was why they needed to move right now. The sooner they got those people out, the better it would be for everyone involved, except of course the scientists they were going to have to deal with.

Them, Ulric wouldn't mind killing. He didn't even care if he wasn't paid for it.

Lawrence cleared his throat. "Do we know how many people they have there?"

"We're not sure. Griffith tried to find out, but now that his father knows he's working with us, he hasn't been talking."

Ulric knocked his knuckles on the table. "Give me an hour with the man, and I'll be able to tell you how many people they have in there and even the color of underwear the scientists like."

Cora laughed. Win didn't. "If you continue behaving this way, I'll make sure you stay home. I'm serious, Ulric. I can't allow you to take part if you're going to be hotheaded. We need to do things the right way, and that means following orders."

"I never said I wouldn't follow orders."

"That's what you've been saying ever since this meeting started."

"I follow orders. You know that. But you've been in one of those labs. You know how it was. Can you honestly tell me you're comfortable leaving those people in there for longer than strictly necessary?"

Win looked down at his notes. "You know I'm not. None of us here is. But this isn't the kind of job we're used to or the kind of job the council had in mind for us when they created our group. The only reason they're allowing us to work with the enforcers is that we were the ones who found out about the lab. And even then, some of the council members aren't happy about the fact that we're going to expose ourselves. They don't want people to know about us, and honestly, I don't either. We do our jobs best when no one knows we exist."

Ulric raked a hand through his hair. "We're not going to be walking in the pride parade with a huge ass banner that says *Council Assassins* or shouting it from the rooftops. We just want to help, and for now, it doesn't look like we're doing anything to do that."

Win's phone rang. Ulric thought he could hear everyone in the room holding their breath as he answered. He knew he did.

"Kameron."

It was a council member. Maybe now was the time. "Of course. We're just in a meeting." Would it kill Win to be a bit more explicit? Ulric was too far away to be able to hear the other side of the conversation, and Win wasn't telling him anything for now.

"How much time do we have?" Win asked.

Ulric straightened in his chair. Maybe this *was* it. Maybe they were finally going to move their asses and do something to help the people stuck in the lab.

"Of course. And I wanted to thank you again for giving us his opportunity. As you know, this is something that's close to our hearts."

Ulric rose from his chair. This really was it.

Win stopped him before he could leave the room to get ready. "Where do you think you're going?"

Dammit. Ulric thought Win would spend a bit more time on the phone. And he was still holding the phone by his ear, so maybe he did. "To get ready."

Win scowled. "Park your ass in the chair. I'll tell you when you can go get ready."

Ulric flopped back into his chair. He idly listened to the rest of the conversation, but he couldn't focus on it. He wanted to go out there, to help. He didn't mind his job, but he'd rather help people than kill them.

He held his breath when Win finally hung up.

Win looked around the table where all the assassins were sitting. Some of them even had their mates there, and everyone stared at him, waiting.

Win nodded. "We're going."

No one cheered, but Ulric felt like it. "When?"

"Now. We're meeting with the enforcers in fifteen minutes. I expect all of you coming with us to be ready in ten minutes."

Ulric only needed five of them.

He wasn't quite sure what to expect from the enforcers when they finally shimmered to the meeting point outside the lab. He was used to working on his own or with his fellow assassins, but not with the team of people in uniform who were staring at them. They probably had no idea who the assassins were, and that was how things should stay. Ulric didn't know what the council had told them, and it didn't matter. He was there to do a job, not to make friends.

The assassins took over. They were good at their jobs, probably better than the enforcers, although Ulric wasn't going to assume anything. Beck only needed five minutes to disable the cameras and security system from home. The enforcers looked stunned, but Ulric ignored them and walked through the doors.

The place looked like an office building. The front doors were all glass, and there was a desk for a security guard in front of them. No one was there right now, though. *Good.* Ulric wanted to kill people who deserved it, and he wouldn't have been able to tell if the guard knew what was happening in the lab.

Instead of going up to where the offices were, they needed to go down. The only way to do that was by using the elevators, and that was where the enforcers came in handy. The elevators were at full capacity as they went down, and with the security system disabled, no one noticed what was happening. Ulric and the others managed to sneak out of the elevators, leaving a few enforcers to guard them. Ulric and the other assassins looked at each other, and Roark, the man in charge since Win was at the warehouse, nodded.

They were off.

Evan disappeared, and Ulric heard more than one enforcer suck in a breath at the sight. He grinned, probably looking like a loon.

The place was full of people. Scientists milled around the labs and various offices, but to Ulric's surprise, there were very few guards. Getting rid of them was a piece of cake. Ulric ran around them using the speed other scientists in another lab had given him, knocking them out before they could even notice that he was there. The other assassins and enforcers gathered the scientists, knocking a few of them out when they tried to defend themselves with scalpels or threatening the prisoners. They managed to rescue a few people from the operating tables in the labs, but Ulric knew there were others.

They just had to find them.

Something was happening. Sky didn't know what it was, but he could hear the sound of people running and screaming outside of the fireproof room he was in. He also noticed the scientists who were watching him from behind the fireproof glass looking at each other warily.

He didn't move.

He was sitting cross-legged in the middle of the room. This was where the scientists had been doing their experiments on him lately. They didn't want to tinker with his DNA anymore, not now that they had what they wanted. They were focused on forcing him to do what they wanted instead, and so far, they hadn't had many results.

Sky was proud of that.

The scientists had tried threatening him, hurting him, even threatening his family. He didn't think they knew where his family was, though. He'd never told them his full name, and he doubted they knew. They would have used that threat sooner if they had. So they didn't have a way to force him to do anything other than hurting him, and he was used to that by now.

"Is something happening?" he asked.

The scientists beyond the glass didn't answer him. He hadn't expected them to, but he did want to know what was going on. Maybe one of the other people had managed to escape. It wasn't the first time that happened, although none of the people had made it out of the lab. Sky wasn't sure where the lab was, but he did know that the only way was the elevators. That meant it was easy enough for the guards to catch anyone who tried to escape.

One of the scientists got up and left the small room behind the glass. The other one turned back to Sky and pushed the button of the intercom to speak with him. "Burn it."

Sky looked at the bunny in the cage. He wasn't sure why the scientists had decided to go from mannequins to animals, but it wasn't going to change anything. Hell, Sky was even less eager to obey than when the only thing he could burn was plastic. There was no way he would set the white bunny on fire.

"Burn it, Sky. You know this is the only way for you to make it out of this place."

Sky flipped him the bird.

The scientist—Sky never bothered learning their names because to him, they were all assholes—glared at him. Sky suspected the man wanted to take him back to the operating table so that he could hurt him. And he might. It wouldn't be the first time, but Sky doubted he'd be allowed to.

The door of the smaller room slammed open so hard that Sky heard it even from his fireproof room. His eyes widened when he saw a man step into the small room and make a beeline for the scientist. The scientist tried to run, but the only exit was the door through which the man had come in.

The man wrapped a big hand around the scientist's throat and slammed him against the wall. Sky watched as the scientist struggled, but the man didn't even seem to notice. He shook the scientist a few times, then turned and threw him toward the door. Sky couldn't see what happened there, not from where he was, but he knew better than to stay still. He was a target where he was, in the center of the room.

He scrambled toward the corner. He watched the door

across the room, holding his breath and waiting. He knew someone was going to come in. Whatever was happening, the scientists were getting their asses kicked. Sky would be all for that in any other circumstances, but if someone had finally come to free to prisoners, he was in trouble.

He didn't want to be free. That wasn't entirely true, of course, but he was *afraid* of being free. He was worried he'd hurt people, and he knew that would happen, since he couldn't control his power.

He'd never hated the scientists who'd done this to him more than he did right now.

He finally had the opportunity to leave this place he hated so much, but he couldn't. He couldn't because of what might happen if he did.

The sound of the door unlocking made him jerk. It creaked a bit as it opened, and Sky couldn't look away. A man came in.

This man was smaller than the one who'd thrown the scientist around in the small room. He was short and very blond. He was cute, and Sky wondered what he was doing there.

The man stopped when he noticed Sky. His gaze went from Sky to the bunny in the cage, then back to Sky. He raised his hands, probably trying to make himself look non-threatening. He didn't have to raise his hands for that to happen. He looked like he belonged on the page of the magazine rather than in this lab.

"I'm not here to hurt you," the man said.

He took a step closer, and Sky caught fire.

The man yelped and jumped back. The fire crackled around Sky, and he couldn't have stopped it even if he'd wanted to—and he didn't. The fire meant he could protect himself from whatever was happening.

"Okay, that's impressive. Can you turn it off?" The man asked.

Sky shook his head.

The man grimaced. "Okay. I'm going to guess that you can't control it."

"You need to stay away."

"I can do that for now, but we are here to help you. We are here to get you free."

Sky couldn't be free. He couldn't be released into the world, not when he'd probably end up burning everyone around him. "Leave me alone. Please."

"You're a prisoner. It's not right. But you're free now. We took over this facility, and the scientists and the guards are all in shackles."

"I need to stay here." No matter how little Sky wanted it, he knew it was the best thing for everyone. Maybe not for himself, but he wasn't the one in danger in this situation. He *was* the danger, and he was ready to sacrifice his freedom to make sure no one got hurt.

The man raised his hands again. "We can help you. I promise."

Sky knew the man had to be hot. Sky never felt too hot anymore, but the man was sweating, and he kept looking at the door as if he couldn't wait to escape.

"You just have to allow us to do something to help," the man said.

Sky swallowed. He wanted to say yes. He wanted this man and whoever was here with him to help him. He wanted to be free, to leave this lab and never come back, to never have to think about it again. It was a pointless dream, though. He couldn't go, not when he'd put everyone's life in danger.

"You need to stay away." Saying the words hurt, but it was the right thing to do.

"I'm Lawrence. You can call me Law."

Why was Lawrence introducing himself? Didn't he realize he needed to leave? "I'm Sky."

"Nice to meet you, Sky. Okay, so can I ask what you are? I don't mean this in an offensive way. I'm just trying to find a way to help you."

"I'm human. I *was* human."

"Okay. Do you know what they did to you?"

"I catch fire."

To Sky's surprise, Law smiled. "I noticed that. I also noticed you couldn't control it. I'm going to take a wild guess here and say that your emotions mess with your control of it?"

"Yes. I caught fire because I'm scared."

"And telling you not to be scared probably isn't going to help. Okay, it's not going to be easy, but I think we can find a way around this."

"A way around this? I'm on *fire*. I can't leave this room. This place is safe, so you need to go and leave me here."

"That's not going to happen. We're closing this facility, and that means we leave no one behind, especially not someone who was a prisoner here. Do you want to stay here, or do you think you should because of the fire?"

Sky opened his arms. The fire danced around him, but Law didn't seem to be afraid. "What do you think? I'll burn people if I step foot outside this room. I can't allow that to happen."

Law smiled again. "Leave it to me."

It wasn't like Sky had a choice, did he?

Ulric pushed the scientist to his knees. The man stumbled as he fell, but Ulric didn't attempt to keep him upright. None of the people he and the others had caught tonight deserved that kind of regard. They were monsters, plain and simple, even though there were human.

Ulric had expected what he'd found in the cells and the operating rooms. He'd been through this once already, and that time, he'd been one of those who got rescued. He wasn't this time, and he was glad he could help these people. No one deserved to be locked in a cell. No one deserved to be turned into something they were never meant to be. Ulric was lucky enough he'd gotten used to his new ability. All the assassins had, and thanks to those abilities, they'd found a job and a makeshift family. Not everyone would be so lucky, though.

And not everyone was made to be an assassin.

Killing people, even though they deserved it, was hard. What Ulric and the other assassins did was done in cold blood. They didn't act under the fire of emotions, and they didn't have regrets. Ulric had learned a long time ago not to have them. The people he and the others killed didn't deserve to be thought about twice once they were dead. They hurt and killed vulnerable people, children, and *death* was the only thing they deserved.

"Is that it?" Roark asked.

They'd gathered everyone in the closest room big enough by the elevators. There were going to need easy access once they started getting people out of there, but none of them wanted the prisoners to see the people who had tortured them while they finally walked toward freedom and safety. Once all of them were out and in healers' hands, the enforcers would get the scientists and guards away and shimmer them to the council jail. They would have done that already, but of course, the entire floor was shielded to Nix.

Cora nodded. "I asked a few enforcers to do one last check on this building, but I think we got all the bad guys out."

"The prisoners?"

"We left them in the cells as you ordered."

It had been hard. Ulric had walked into a few cells to try to reassure the prisoners, and he'd wanted to take those people to freedom, but it was safer for them to stay where they were while the enforcers and the assassins took care of their jailers.

Now that the bad guys were locked up, they were going to be able to free the prisoners, and Ulric couldn't wait. He still remembered how it felt, and he wanted to give that to someone else, to reassure them and show them they could make it, that they didn't have to be what the scientists and the people paying them had planned for them to be.

Lawrence appeared at the door. He was alone, but then all the bad guys were already in the room. He saw Roark and made a beeline for him. "We have a problem."

Roark frowned. "A problem?"

"One of the prisoners. I went into this room, and the scientists were forcing him to try to set a bunny on fire, I think. I tried talking to him, and I don't know what the scientists did to him, but he's on fire."

Roark's eyes widened. "We need to evacuate."

Lawrence shook his head. "That's not why I'm here. Sky is in a fireproof room. Everyone here is safe, I promise. But the problem is that Sky can't turn the fire off. From what I understand, his ability to catch fire is linked to his emotions. When he feels strongly, *poof.*"

Ulric blinked. "Poof?"

Lawrence shrugged. "Pretty much. I have no idea how it happened or what was done to him, but since Cora can control fire, I thought she might be able to help him."

Roark nodded. "All right. You take Cora and go to him, maybe Tony, too, since his ability with ice and cold could be useful. The rest of us will get everyone out. We'll let you know when it's safe to take him out of the fireproof room."

Ulric had to see this. Since Roark hadn't given him a direct order, he followed Lawrence, Cora, and Tony out of the room. They had to walk toward the back of the floor, and Ulric recognized it. He'd walked into a small room with two scientists watching something through a glass earlier. He'd knocked them out and had dragged them to the elevators, but he hadn't stopped to check through the glass because Lawrence had been there. He should have known better than to ignore it, and he hated himself for not trying to do something for this Sky guy. Not that he could have done much since fire wasn't his forte, but he could have tried to reassure Sky.

The guy was on fire. Lawrence had already explained that, but Ulric hadn't expected it to look like this. What looked like a man was curled up in the corner of the room, his knees against his chest. Ulric couldn't see much of Sky, since he was on fire, but he looked on the smaller side, or maybe that was because he was sitting on the floor curled up into a ball.

A few enforcers had followed them into the room, but thankfully, they stayed by the door. Their eyes were wide, and Ulric knew he'd have looked very much like them if he hadn't seen Cora deal with fire already. But he knew what she could do, and he suspected that Sky was like her. She was the best person to help him, so Ulric stayed at a distance. He was close enough to intervene if something went wrong, but not so close that Sky would freak out because of him. Tony stood next to him, his gaze fixed on Sky and Cora as she stepped closer. He was tense, ready to step in just like Ulric was.

"Hi. I'm Cora."

It was hard to say if Sky was looking at her. His face was turned toward her, so Ulric thought he was.

"You need to leave," Sky said.

"I'm not going anywhere. I can help you. I promise."

"You don't understand. I can't turn it off. I'm dangerous."

He shrank against the wall when Cora moved even closer. She reached for him, and Ulric held his breath even though he knew nothing would happen to her. He heard the enforcers behind him cry out, but it was too late. Cora had taken Sky's hand, and nothing had happened to her. She didn't seem to be in pain, because she wasn't. She could create fire and control it, and if she wanted, she could get her entire body to catch fire, just like Sky's. She was different from him because she had control over it, but that had come in time.

"How?" Sky asked. There was wonder in his voice, the same wonder Ulric felt watching them. No matter how used he was to Cora's ability, it was always incredible to watch her use it.

Cora smiled. "I told you I can help you. I was like you once. I learned control, and you can, too."

Sky snorted. "Not in time to get out of here. I'm ready to bet it's not something you learned in minutes."

"You're right. It's not. But we're not going to leave you here. I want to sedate you."

Sky tried to press harder against the wall, but there was nowhere for him to go. "I don't want to be sedated."

"I know that's what the scientists who did this to you did. I also know you don't know if you can trust us. I can make as many promises as I want, but it's not going to change that fact. You'll have to trust me. I promise I'll teach you control as soon as you're out of here. But you have to get out of here first, and that won't happen if you're still on fire. I can help you calm down, but with everything happening, I doubt you'll manage. The only way out for you right now is to be sedated."

Ulric thought Sky was going to say no. He would have if he'd been in Sky's place. The last thing he would have wanted when he'd been freed from the lab was to be knocked out. Just thinking about it would have terrified him.

But Sky was stronger than him. He took a moment to think about it, then he nodded. "Promise you'll make sure I don't hurt anyone."

"Of course. But if your ability is anything like mine, you won't catch fire if you're not conscious."

"I've never woken up on fire."

"Then you won't this time, either."

Cora reached for her waist. She took out a syringe and held

it up. "I'm going to need you to focus on putting the fire out in your arm. I know it's hard, but this is going to melt otherwise."

Ulric held his breath as Cora walked Sky through it. He was surprised that Sky managed, and soon after, he was asleep. Cora leaned back, and her shoulders relaxed. She turned toward Tony and Ulric. "I need one of you to carry him."

Ulric stepped forward. The enforcers did, too, but Ulric glared at them until they stepped back again. He reached Cora and crouched next to her. "I'll do it."

Cora looked as tired as Ulric felt. "Thank you."

Ulric reached for Sky. Now that he could see the man, he couldn't help but notice how good he looked. He had long brown tangled hair, and while shorter than Ulric, it wasn't by much. He was too thin, which wasn't surprising considering he had to have been in the lab for a while. Ulric wouldn't have a hard time carrying him.

The smell hit him when he leaned over Sky. Sky smelled of smoke, of something wild and untamable, and he smelled of Ulric's mate.

CHAPTER TWO

This wasn't the first time Sky didn't know where he was when he woke up.

It was hard to resist the urge to flail and try to run, especially with his heart racing in his chest. Sky swallowed and looked around. He was in a hospital, maybe, or an infirmary. He couldn't hear anything outside the room, so probably not a hospital. There was still a distinct hospital smell and feeling to the room, though, and it made Sky's stomach churn.

He swallowed again, but his mouth was dry. He tried to move his legs and arms, relieved when he could. The last time he'd woken up in a hospital, he'd been tied to the bed.

"Oh, you're awake."

Sky jerked and tried to roll off the bed. Two hands closed around his arms, and panic filled his chest.

"Please, calm down. I'm not going to hurt you, and I would rather not have to sedate you again. You're safe here. I promise."

The hands disappeared. Sky was free, and he used that freedom to roll off the bed and crouch next to the wall. He looked around, trying to find an exit, and his gaze stopped on the man who'd been holding him.

The man wore scrubs. He was taller than Sky by a few inches, from what Sky could see, and his glasses and messy reddish-brown hair helped make him look harmless. He didn't reach for Sky again, not even to help him up, and Sky felt himself relax.

He remembered now. He remembered the woman who'd

told him she was like him. He remembered her telling him she would help him. "Where is she?" he asked.

"You mean Cora? She was here earlier, but she had to leave. Paperwork."

Sky blinked. "Paperwork?"

"Yes. You know, from your rescue. Well, yours and everyone else's in the lab. The council expects all the paperwork to be in order when we do this kind of thing."

Sky looked around again, but they were alone. "Where are we?"

"I'm not sure I should be the one telling you that."

Sky snorted. "Because that's not making me feel anxious."

The man laughed. "You're going to fit right in." He held his hand out. "I'm Rocco. I know your name is Sky, but that's about all I know about you. I haven't been over your files yet. I wanted to talk to you first, see if it was okay with you if I did."

Sky slowly rose. He stayed by the wall, but he didn't think Rocco was a danger to him. If he'd been like the doctors in the lab, he'd have tied Sky to the bed, and he wouldn't have introduced himself. Besides, he didn't feel the same way. He was calm and relaxed, even though he was obviously worried about Sky.

Rocco cleared his throat. "I'm going to call someone."

Sky wasn't sure he wanted that to happen. "Wait."

Rocco hadn't moved yet. Sky wasn't sure what to tell him. He thought it was quite evident that he was afraid, but his fear didn't mean he would be allowed to stay here. He didn't know who had rescued him from the lab, or where he was. He didn't know what would happen to him. He needed to find out, and that wasn't going to happen if he stayed where he was and begged Rocco not to bring anyone else in.

Sky breathed in and out a few times to calm himself. The last thing he needed was to catch fire. He didn't know whether he was in danger or not, but he was leaning toward not. He'd learned to trust his instincts when he'd been in the lab, and so far, they seemed to be working fine.

"Can you really not tell me anything?" he asked.

"I don't think I'm the right man for that."

"Why are you here with me, then?"

"Because I'm a doctor, and you're in my infirmary. As I said, I didn't go over the files that were brought in with you, even though they would have helped me treat you."

"I was sedated."

"I know. I wanted to make sure you were okay beyond the sedation, though. But I have no idea what you were to begin with, or what was done to you in the lab. If you give me the go-ahead, I'll check your files."

"Can you take the fire away?"

Rocco grimaced. "I want to say yes, but I doubt it. Cora has the same ability as you, and I haven't been able to take it away from her. She's learned to control it, though, so I wouldn't worry too much if I were you."

These people didn't seem to understand that Sky was more worried for them than he was for himself. "Am I safe here?"

"Of course you're. You're safe in the entire house, but I understand if you'd rather stick to the infirmary for now. Let me call Cora and Tony. They'll be able to tell you more, since they talked with the people in charge."

"I was human." Sky doubted that knowing that was going to help, but Rocco was a doctor, and he probably needed to know. He might be able to find a way to keep the fire in. Maybe he could keep Sky sedated. That sounded like the best idea considering Sky didn't know where he was or how many people were in the house. He wanted answers first, though. He *needed* them.

Rocco nodded. "All right. I have your permission to check on your files?"

"Yes. I have no idea what's in them, though."

"That doesn't matter. I've been over files from this kind of lab more than once, so I know what to expect, and I know what to look for. I just want to make sure you're healthy and that there's nothing I need to do to keep you that way."

Skype didn't think that being able to catch fire was healthy, but he didn't say it. He understood what Rocco meant. Being a smart ass wasn't going to help anyone, least of all him.

He sat back on the bed while Rocco disappeared through a side door. The door stayed open, and Sky could hear Rocco talk to someone, no doubt on the phone. He was curious to find out where he was, and who had decided it was a good idea to take him to a place where people lived. He hadn't missed the way Rocco had said this was a house, even though the infirmary looked professional. That meant people lived there, and that Sky might be a danger to them.

He was surprised he hadn't caught fire as soon as he'd opened his eyes, or when Rocco had touched him. He'd been frightened enough to, but maybe there was still some of that stuff they'd used to sedate him in his bloodstream, enough for him not to be able to set everything on fire.

Sky was relieved when the woman from the lab walked through the big doors at the end of the room. They were the kind of doors that only needed to be pushed, just like in a hospital.

She wasn't alone, but Sky recognized the men with her. They'd been there when she'd sedated him, and he hoped that the fact that they hadn't hurt him then meant they wouldn't now. They stopped at the foot of Sky's bed. He was glad for the space they left between them.

The woman—Cora—smiled. "Glad to see you're awake and well."

Sky chuckled. "I don't know about well, but I am awake. I tried asking the doctor where I was, but he didn't want to answer."

"Rocco is always careful. But I'm allowed to tell you where you are, so you don't have to worry about that." She looked at the two men that bracketed her, then back at Sky. "You know about the shifter council."

"Of course."

"You were rescued from the lab you were in during one of our raids. We arrested the scientists and the guards, and rescued the prisoners, including you."

"Are they here, too?" Sky doubted it, since there was no one but him in the infirmary, but he had to ask. He had to know if he was putting people in danger.

"No. You're a special case. They were taken to the hospital. But I knew you would need me, and the council agreed to allow us to teach you here."

Sky threw his hands in the air. "You still haven't told me where *here* is."

"I was getting to that. Over the past decades, the council has picked people like you and me, who were changed and have a special ability. We were asked if we wanted to be part of the council assassins."

"Assassins?" That didn't sound good.

"It's exactly what you think. We take care of humans and shifters both. Drug dealers, human traffickers, pedophiles. Anything you can think of. Where the official justice cannot reach, we go."

"You're professional killers."

"We are. The fact that you're here doesn't mean you have to become one. You're welcome to leave anytime you want. But I'd like you to stay, at least while I teach you control."

Sky wasn't going anywhere. He needed to learn control if he didn't want to set the world on fire, and he didn't care who taught it to him. He tilted this chin toward the two men. "What about them?"

"Tony controls ice and cold. He might be useful if you lose control."

"And him?" Sky had a hard time looking away from the other guy. His brown hair was as messy as Rocco's had been, although in his case, it didn't look like it was on purpose. The freckles on his nose and cheeks were adorable, and Sky found himself wondering if he'd be able to count them.

The man stepped forward, jarring Sky out of those thoughts. "I'm Ulric. I'm here because you're my mate."

Ulric probably should have found another way to tell Sky that. The poor man didn't know where he was, or what was going to happen to him, and Ulric had just dumped another shock on him. He hadn't known how else to do it, though. Sky needed to know they were mates, or at least, Ulric thought so.

A few people had tried to dissuade him from telling Sky today. They thought it would be better for Sky to grow used to the idea that he was living with the council assassins and that he needed to learn control from one of them. Ulric couldn't deny Sky had already had enough shocks today. He'd been rescued from the lab, he'd been sedated, and he'd woken up in a place he didn't know, surrounded by people he'd never seen before.

Ulric couldn't have hidden it, though. He had no idea what Sky thought about it, but he hoped that knowing there was someone in his corner would help. He'd seen how his friends had reacted to finding their mates. None of them had had an easy time with it or with the situation they'd been in when it had happened, but Ulric had seen how much being aware that they weren't alone had helped. That was all Ulric wanted for Sky.

Sky looked at him. "Your mate?"

Ulric prayed Sky wasn't about to say he didn't want

anything to do with him. "Yes. I knew as soon as I volunteered to help to carry you out."

"When I was unconscious."

"Yes. Cora needed help. I wanted to help."

"And you smelled me."

"Yes. You smell like smoke and fire." Ulric thought this was a good thing. He liked it. He didn't know if Sky shared that opinion.

Sky shook his head. "I'm glad you told me rather than keeping it to yourself, but I'm not sure what you expect from me."

"Nothing."

Sky didn't look convinced. "You just said I'm your mate. I know how that works."

"Of course you do, but that doesn't mean we have to mate right away, or even at all. I don't expect anything from you, promise. I understand you've been through a lot, more than most people. We all understand. We were all like you once, liberated from a lab and with powers we didn't have before. We were all lost."

Sky tugged on a strand of his hair. "I find it hard to believe."

Ulric took a chance and dragged one of the chairs closer to Sky's bed. Sky eyed him and slid his legs under the sheet as if it was a shield.

Ulric wasn't offended. Like he'd told Sky, he knew what he was going through. He sat on the chair and leaned closer, but not close enough to touch Sky. "Your life is a mess right now. Even though I don't know anything about you, that, I know. You spent who knows how long in a lab. You were experimented on. You were changed. You're not human anymore, and you don't know how to deal with that. You need to learn control. You're in a strange place with strange people, and one of them just told you you're his mate. I'd be an asshole if

I expected you to fall in love with me right away, or even to like me. I want to be there for you because I know how hard this is going to be, but that's it."

Ulric couldn't read Sky's expression, but it didn't matter. He'd told Sky what he wanted to tell him, and now, he'd have to wait.

Rocco chose that moment to come out of his office, and Ulric was grateful. They could all use a little distraction.

Rocco was holding a small stack of files, and he dropped it onto the bed next to Sky's. "I know you probably don't want anyone to touch you right now, but I'd like to examine your eyes."

Ulric didn't miss the way Sky leaned back, so he was surprised when his mate nodded. Rocco moved closer, shining his little light into Sky's eyes. It was obvious he was trying hard not to touch Sky, and Ulric was grateful. Sky wasn't comfortable, just like they'd all expected, and he needed space.

Rocco put his light away. "Do you have strange marks on your skin? Things that weren't there when you were human?"

Sky frowned. "How do you know? Did you examine me?"

"I didn't. I didn't touch you beyond making sure you were comfortable and still sedated. But I quickly went over your files, and I know what happened. I know what they did to you. You're more similar to Cora then I thought possible."

Ulric leaned forward. Cora was a demon—an agrona demon—the most powerful kind there was. She'd told him that agrona demons had the power to control fire, but not the way she could now. The scientists had manipulated her DNA to the point where she could now turn her entire body to fire, like Sky.

Ulric had no idea how the scientists did that. He'd never understood it, no matter how many times Rocco had tried to explain it. It was too complicated for him, and he had no interest in knowing how to do it. But now that Rocco had mentioned it, it was hard to ignore Sky's eyes. Ulric didn't know what color they'd been before, but now, they were a swirling black and green, unlike Cora, who had solid black eyes.

"I don't understand," Sky said. He sounded lost, and Ulric wished there were something he could do to help him.

He wasn't sure how Sky would react, but he slid a hand under the sheet toward Sky's legs and cupped one of Sky's naked ankles. Sky jerked and looked at Ulric, but he didn't try to pull his leg away. Ulric gently squeezed, and Sky gave him a tiny smile before turning his attention back to Rocco.

"Your DNA was spliced with agrona demon DNA. That's why you're not fully human anymore. You're partly demon," Rocco explained.

"I barely know anything about demons."

"No one does. They keep to themselves, which is why the fact that Cora is here to help you is a small miracle. You're like her now. Not entirely demon, of course, but you share the same power. She can help you learn control, so you don't hurt yourself or anyone else."

"I didn't expect this, but of course, I'll help," Cora said.

Ulric relaxed. He'd known Cora would help anyway, but maybe being similar to her would help Sky. She was the only demon in the house, and he needed help, both to learn control and understand what he was now. Ulric had been a wolf shifter before he was caught. He now had the ability of super-speed, and while it had been hard to deal with, he'd already known how being different felt. It had still taken him a while to get used to it, of course, and he could imagine how hard it would be for Sky, who'd been human.

"Thank you," Sky murmured. "But I'm not sure that keeping me here is a good idea. Since you know what I can do, you know how dangerous I am for other people."

"Don't worry about that. I didn't have control when I first got here, either. I never set the house on fire. I had a special fireproof bedroom I moved out of a while ago. You can have it for as long as you want or need it."

"When do we start?" He was eager, and Ulric liked that.

Sky knew how dangerous he was, and he wanted to change that. He could have chosen to curl up in a ball and ignore the world. He could have lamented the fact that he was different now and that learning control would be hard. That was what Ulric had done in the beginning. He'd whined about what had happened to him for way too long. But Sky wasn't.

"As soon as possible. But first, I'd like to know how you ended up in the lab. We're asking this question to all the prisoners we found there."

Sky sighed. "I suppose saying no isn't an option."

"No one will force you to talk about it, but finding this lab wasn't something we expected. We thought that time was over, and we're trying to find out how it happened."

"I don't know what to tell you. I guess it happened like it usually does. I was snatched off the streets, sedated, and when I woke up, I was in a cell."

Those scientists were lucky they were in cells themselves right now, because Ulric would have torn their balls off their bodies and nailed them to the wall otherwise.

Sky didn't want to think about the time he'd spent in the lab now that he was out of it, but he suspected Cora wouldn't leave him alone until he told her what she wanted to hear.

"And once you were in the cell? What happened?" she asked.

"They kept me there for a while. Then they took me out to the operating room. And don't ask me what they did to me once I was there because I don't know. I remember pain and waking up different. That's all."

A hand squeezed Sky's ankle. He didn't look at Ulric, even though he wanted to. He couldn't understand why Ulric was touching him. Ulric had seen him on fire. He knew Sky could hurt him. Yet it didn't seem to make a difference to him.

Sky had been stunned when Ulric had first sat next to his bed and touched him. He hadn't been quite sure what to think of the gesture, but he was glad for it, even though he was afraid he'd hurt Ulric. Ulric's touch was reassuring, just as much as it was confusing. Sky felt a little panicky knowing Ulric was his mate, or rather, that he was Ulric's mate, but right now, he was so focused on answering Cora's questions and trying not to think about what had been done to him that it was easy to push that feeling away. The memories were enough to eclipse any other emotion.

Sky knew he had to think about this mate thing. He had no idea how to handle it, though. He was happy about Ulric finding him, both for him and Ulric, but he knew it would be better for everyone if he stayed away. He should leave this place, but he wouldn't, not if Cora could help him.

"Do you think you could recognize the people who took you?"

Sky wished he could. "Their faces were covered. They knew what they were doing, and I doubt anyone in the lab could recognize them. The only people I could help you with arc the scientists and the guards in the lab. I've never saw those men who took me from the street again." And he didn't want to see them. He'd already killed a guard, and even though he hadn't done it on purpose, he couldn't be sure he wouldn't hurt those men if their paths crossed again.

He cleared his throat. "I have something to tell you." They deserved to know he was a killer. He didn't know what they would think of him after he told them, but he hoped they wouldn't kick his ass out. They were professional killers.

They weren't innocent, just like he wasn't innocent either, not anymore.

Ulric squeezed Sky's ankle again. "What is it?" he asked, and Sky found himself wishing he could lean against Ulric, use his warmth and presence to comfort himself. "You can tell us anything. We won't judge."

How could Sky be sure of that? But either way, whether they judged him or not, he had to tell them. "I killed a man — a guard. I didn't mean to, but he came in my cell, and he was going to hurt me, and I couldn't control my ability then either. I — he reached for me and grabbed my arm, and I caught fire." Sky still remembered the smell. He didn't think he would ever forget it, or that he'd be able to eat bacon again.

Ulric patted Sky's leg. "It was an accident."

"How do you know?"

"You just said yourself that he was going to hurt you, and he was the one who grabbed you. It sounds to me like self-defense, but I understand how you might blame yourself for it."

"You do?"

Ulric glared. "I might be a professional assassin, but that doesn't mean I don't have feelings. I feel remorse like everyone else. I blame myself for things just like you do."

Sky didn't want him to take his hand away. The thought was enough for the panic to fill his chest, so he scrambled to apologize. "I'm sorry. That's not what I meant."

Ulric shrugged. "It's okay. You're confused and wondering what's going to happen to you. You might not be in physical pain, but everything that was done to you in the lab is going to have consequences, repercussions. We're here to help you go through them, to learn to deal with them and find a way to get your life in order."

Sky wanted to believe him. He knew that was why he and the others were here, but he still doubted they could help.

"Are you sure you can teach me control?" he asked, looking back at Cora.

She reached for him, but she didn't touch him. Instead, her hand caught fire.

Sky jerked back before he could think about it. Nothing would happen to him even if she touched him, but it was instinct.

"Rocco told you we share the same powers. That's because we now share DNA. You're partly a demon. That makes you family, even though we've never met each other before. You won't find a lot of demons ready to help you, but I am."

Sky wanted to ask why most demons wouldn't help him, why she was the first demon he met, but he had more important things to focus on right now. "How do you do that?"

She closed her hand, and the fire disappeared. "Do what?"

"Focus the fire in your hand. Control the moment it turns on and the moment it turns off."

"You're not ready to start training," Rocco intervened. "You're too thin. You need food and rest."

"I need to start training. Don't you understand how dangerous I am?"

Rocco crossed his arms over his chest, and Sky knew he wouldn't be allowed to do anything until the man gave him the go-ahead. "We are *all* dangerous here. You're nothing different or new from what I've seen and dealt with already."

"I could set the entire building on fire."

"I know. That's why I won't object to you moving to Cora's old room, even though I'd rather keep you here to make sure you're okay."

Sky supposed that was better than nothing. "I *am* okay. The scientists stopped touching me when they realized what I could do. That's when they started trying to train me."

"And you didn't learn from them?" Cora asked.

There was no condemnation in her voice, but Sky couldn't

help but hear it anyway. "They wanted me to kill on command. Do you remember the cage that was in the cell you found me in? That's what training was with them. I had to focus and set the bunny on fire. There's no way I'm killing anything or anyone to learn control. If that's your idea of training, this isn't going to work."

Cora rolled her eyes. "It's not. Don't worry. We're not going to have you kill rabbits."

That was a relief, much more than Sky would've expected. He needed to learn not to hurt people, and that wouldn't happen if his training consisted in hurting people. "How is it going to work, then? Or can I not ask that?" he asked, looking at Rocco. The doctor wasn't going to allow him to start training, but he needed to know what was going to happen. He needed to have a goal to work toward to.

"We'll have to use your bedroom. It's fireproof, so whatever happens in there won't be a problem. Or we could go to the roof, which is another place where I used to train. The problem with the roof is that people could see us, and we don't want that."

Obviously not.

"So Tony and I will come to your room as soon as Rocco says we can," Cora continued. "Tony will be there mostly in case something happens. If you lose control or something like that."

Sky was curious about the man. Tony hadn't spoken to him yet, and he couldn't help but wonder why that was. "I know you said Tony can control the cold, but I'm not quite sure what you meant."

Cora looked back at Tony, who grinned. It made him look more approachable, which was a plus if Sky was going to spend any length of time with him. Tony reached for Sky, and before Sky could tell him to fuck off, he wrapped his fingers around Sky's wrist. Sky felt the panic bubble and rise to his skin, but before anything could happen, cold invaded him. It pushed back the fire, even though Sky could still feel it there, just under the surface.

Tony smiled. "That's how I'm going to help. I can't do jack shit for the control, even though I had to learn it, too, but this, I can do."

Maybe Sky had a chance after all.

Ulric was relieved when Cora, Tony, and Rocco left the room. He could see from Sky's expression that he was overwhelmed, and he felt guilty. He knew he was part of the reason. He probably shouldn't have told Sky they were mates the way he had, at least for now. He should have waited until Sky was more settled, but he'd been afraid.

It was evident that Sky didn't feel comfortable, and Ulric didn't want him to leave. He didn't know if knowing they were mates was going to keep Sky here, but he hoped it would help, and not just because he didn't want to lose him right after finding him.

Sky needed help. It wasn't a bad thing, but it was apparent Sky wasn't happy with that. Ulric suspected it was more because Sky was afraid that he'd hurt people than because he wanted to leave, but he wasn't taking any chances.

He finally slid his hand away from Sky's ankle and instantly missed the contact. "Is there anything else you want to know before I show you Cora's old room?" he asked. He should probably call it Sky's room now to make Sky feel more like he was home. He wouldn't be able to leave for a while, and Ulric wanted him to feel comfortable, to become part of their family.

Sky shook his head. Cora had left him a hair tie before leaving, and he'd pulled up the brown mass into a messy bun. Strands had ready escaped it and framed his face.

He looked painfully young, and Ulric wondered how old

34

he was.

"I think I have everything for now. I'll probably have more questions about training later, but not before we start."

"I meant about everything," Ulric said. "Not only training, but what happened with the lab and the scientists, or where you are, or even if you want to call your family. I can do that."

Ulric remembered all too well how it felt to be free of the lab. The first thing he'd thought was that he wanted to strangle the scientists and the guards who'd hurt him with his bare hands. The second had been that he needed to call his family because they were no doubt frantic.

Sky's eyes widened, and he pressed back against the pillows. "I don't want you to call my parents."

Ulric blinked. He hadn't expected that. "Are you sure? They'll probably be relieved to find out you're okay."

"And they'd want me to come home, but I can't do that."

Of course. Ulric should've known. Sky was so worried about hurting people that he wouldn't want to leave the fireproof room until he had at least some control over his new ability. He wouldn't want to put his family in danger by contacting them now. And he was probably right when he said that his family would want to see him. Ulric wasn't sure how long Sky had been gone from their lives, but even a week would have been too long for them.

He raised his hands. "I won't call them if you don't want me to. I promise."

Sky relaxed again. "Thank you. Rocco said I could leave the infirmary."

Ulric suspected Rocco would have been more comfortable if Sky stayed for at least one night. He took his people's health seriously, and Sky was one of them now. But it would be safer for everyone, including Sky, if he moved into Cora's old fireproof room tonight. He'd already spent the entire day in the infirmary, and that had been allowed because he'd been unconscious. He wasn't anymore, which meant he might be dangerous. Most assassins would be able to deal with that, but they weren't the only ones who lived in the house anymore. They had to think of the human mates, and that meant isolating Sky until he had enough control not to catch fire spontaneously.

He nodded. "You can. Come on. I'll walk you to your new bedroom." And he'd explain how the place worked. Most humans didn't live in big familial units the way the assassins did. It would take a while for Sky to become used to it, although after the lab, it would be a step up.

Sky was wearing a hospital gown, but Ulric knew where Rocco kept the spare clothes. He'd had to patch up the assassins enough times to know that sometimes they needed extra clothes. It was that or sending them back to their rooms naked, and no one wanted to see North's prickly ass hanging out.

Sky seemed to realize his problem, and his cheeks flushed. He pulled the sheet around his shoulders and looked away. He was too adorable for Ulric's heart, dammit.

Ulric cleared his throat. "Stay in bed. I'll be right back."

He grabbed the clothes from the dresser by the door and left them on the bed before leaving the infirmary to wait outside. It wasn't anything fancy, just a pair of sweatpants and a white t-shirt, but at least Sky would be covered. He probably already felt terrible enough not to want to walk around a house he didn't know and people he'd never met half-naked.

Ulric jumped a bit when the infirmary door opened, but it was just Sky. He'd put on the clothes, including the thick socks Ulric had taken out for him. He looked like a kid who was wearing his father's clothes. Because of the many big men living in the house and needing the infirmary regularly, Rocco only kept bigger sizes. Ulric was going to have to buy Sky new clothes, things in which he could feel more comfortable. That could wait for a few days, though. Sky was going to want to choose his own clothes, and he was in the wrong frame of mind to do that now.

Sky's eyes were wide as Ulric led him through the house. Cora's old room wasn't part of the main house. It was linked to it through the garage, but Win and the council had thought it more secure for it to be separate. That way, if she set her room on fire, everyone in the warehouse would be safe, but she could still feel like she was part of their lives. That had worked for her, and Ulric hoped it would work for Sky.

"What is this place?" Sky asked on their way down the stairs.

"It's our lair. Our home. All of us live here because it's safer this way, so it has to be big."

"There's big, and then there's *big*."

Ulric laughed. "And you haven't seen the upper levels yet. We had to expand when people kept meeting their mates."

Sky snuck a glance at Ulric. "Are there a lot of them here? Mates, I mean."

"Not until recently. We had no idea how to handle it when Roark met Noel. This place was only supposed to be for the council assassins, and there was Roark, in love with a human. But we made things work. We're lucky that so far, all the mates have agreed to move in with us."

"That's what you expect from me?"

"I told you, I don't expect anything from you. You're free to do as you want." Even though it would break Ulric's heart if Sky decided to leave. He would understand, though. Just like all the other assassins, he knew what Sky was going through. He knew how confusing and overwhelming everything was for him right now. The only thing he could do was to be there for Sky and let him find his way in his new life.

"I can't leave yet."

"You can if you want to, but I think we all agree that you

should stay and train with Cora." And hopefully by the time Sky had his ability under control, he'd have gotten to know Ulric, and he would agree to at least try. That was all Ulric wanted. He wanted them to try to be together. He wanted the happiness most of his friends had, for both of them.

They walked across the length of the garage to a door on the other side of it. Sky looked confused until Ulric opened the door and ushered him into the hallway, then through the suite's front door. It was probably nothing like he expected.

Cora hadn't just had a room. She had a small suite, with a second bedroom and a small living room. She'd needed the space as much as she'd needed to feel part of their family. The rooms were still filled with cheap but comfortable furniture. It was nothing they couldn't lose in case of a fire, and once the doors were closed, the garage and the warehouse were isolated. That meant that even if Sky caught fire and burned everything in the suite, the fire wouldn't reach the house.

Ulric walked in, closed the door behind them, and gestured to the door that had been Cora's. "That's the master bedroom and the guest room. You're free to choose which one you prefer, of course, but I think you'll be more comfortable in the biggest one."

"What about the guestroom?"

"I'll be moving in." Ulric knew Sky wouldn't be happy about that because it would put him in danger, but he didn't care. He wasn't leaving Sky on his own, not when his life had once again been flipped upside down.

CHAPTER THREE

Sky was making progress, but he knew it wasn't enough. He'd been there for a week, living with the assassins—and God, he hated calling them that. They didn't feel like family yet to him, but Cora and Tony had become friends, or at least Sky felt that way. And Ulric—Sky had no idea what to do with the man.

Ulric didn't seem to care about his own safety. He'd wanted to move into the guestroom of the fireproof suite even though Sky had told him no. He wouldn't listen when Sky told him it would be safer for him to keep his distance. Of course, being an assassin probably meant he never bothered thinking about his safety. Sky didn't know how to get through to him, and he'd stopped trying three days in. Ulric wouldn't do anything Ulric didn't want to do, and that included keeping his distance with Sky. The only way Sky had found that worked was to go through Win, which was exactly what he'd done and why Ulric wasn't sleeping in the guest room no matter how much he'd whined about it.

Besides Sky had other things to focus on.

Cora poked him on the cheek. "You're not focusing."

Sky gritted his teeth. "It's kind of hard to do that when you keep poking me."

Cora was like an older sister. Sky knew he had to listen to her because she knew what she was talking about, but that didn't make her any less annoying. She'd showed him the first day after Sky had moved into her old suite of rooms. She'd come, along with Tony, to talk about what Sky's training was going to consist of. She'd given him a small show, setting various parts of her body on fire and turning it off. She'd even set fire to a few candles that had been on the coffee table. It had been impressive, and Sky wasn't sure if he would ever be able to do that. The only thing he could set on fire was himself, and that was more than enough for him. He wouldn't mind using a lighter if he needed to light candles.

"I'm poking you because you're not focusing. Not the other way around."

"Are you sure about that?"

Tony guffawed. "He's thinking about Ulric."

Sky didn't want to blush, but he *had* been thinking about Ulric. He didn't like that he was so transparent, even though it was to Tony. "Of course I'm thinking about him. He still refuses to go back to his bedroom."

Cora tsked. "You won't be able to convince him to do that. You know it. You might as well stop."

She made it sound easy, but every moment Ulric spent with Sky put his life in danger. Sky would never forgive himself if he hurt anyone, but least of all, Ulric. He didn't know if it was because they were mates, but Ulric had seemingly decided he was going to be Sky's guide and anchor in this new life of his. Sky didn't mind, not entirely. He did feel like he needed help to navigate his ability, the house, and all the people who lived there, and he wanted to spend more time with Ulric and get to know him. But at the same time, he was terrified.

Cora and Tony were safe around him. Cora wouldn't be hurt even if Sky accidentally set her on fire. Tony might, but he was fast enough that he could cool himself and most of the room in seconds.

Ulric, though, had no way to fight Sky's ability. He'd get burned if Sky lost control, and Sky couldn't bear to think about it. He didn't care if it was because they were mates or because Ulric was a good man. Whatever the reason, he didn't want Ulric to get hurt.

"You know, there's one way to be sure you won't hurt Ulric," Cora said.

Sky frowned. "There is?"

"You could learn control. That way, you won't catch fire when he finally gets you into bed."

"Cora!" If Sky hadn't been blushing before, he certainly was now.

"What? You're his mate. You live together. Am I supposed to think you're not getting it on, or that you wouldn't be if you weren't too afraid to hurt him?"

"We barely know each other." Not that Sky's cock cared about that, but he wasn't about to tell Cora. He'd thought he'd never get hard again after the lab, but sharing his living spaces with Ulric had shown him how wrong he'd been. Ulric tested Sky's control, and not just the weak one he had over his ability.

Sky wanted him, dammit. He wanted him in his bed and his life, and he couldn't have that until he got himself under control.

"Barely knowing each other doesn't mean you don't want to bone him."

Sky groaned. "This is like talking about sex with my mother. Can you please stop?"

Cora scowled at him. "I'm not nearly old enough to be your mother, asshole. Now focus and set your hand on fire."

Sky ignored Tony's snickering and did what he'd been told. Or at least, he tried to. He'd never been able to set only part of his body on fire. Every time he'd caught fire, his entire body had done so. He'd never been able to do it on command. He still wasn't, no matter how hard he focused on his hands.

Cora sighed. "This isn't working."

Sky's shoulders slumped. "I'm sorry."

"You shouldn't be. I'm not surprised it's not working. It took me a few weeks to manage to focus the fire in my hand, and even longer to not catch fire every time I felt strongly about something. You're doing well, considering."

Sky didn't feel like he was. He wanted to start living again, to get back everything the lab and the scientists had taken from him, but he couldn't do that if he couldn't leave his bedroom.

Cora tapped her fingers tips on the coffee table and peered at Sky in a way that told him she was planning something. He probably wasn't going to like it. "You know what your problem is?" she asked.

Sky rolled his eyes. "No, but I bet you're about to tell me."

"Damn right I am. Your problem is that you're isolating yourself."

"If you remember, there's a good reason for that."

To Sky's surprise, Tony interrupted their conversation. "What Cora is trying to say is that you need people."

"I have the two of you." And Ulric since he'd apparently decided he wouldn't mind getting crispy.

"You do, but there are a lot of people out there who want to meet you. Did you know that Graham sets a plate for you at the table every night?"

Sky hadn't, even though he knew who Graham was. Ulric talked about his family and his friends all the time, and Sky felt like he knew all of them. "I can't go to dinner. I can't risk it."

"But staying here on your own isn't doing you any good. Being with others will help you relax, and that will make it easier for you to control your ability, because you won't be obsessing over it. You need a distraction."

"A distraction would be deadly."

Cora threw her hands in the air. "Listen to him, Sky. This isn't working. You need to change something if you want to finally be able to take a step forward."

"I'll try harder."

"You're already trying as hard as you can. Your will isn't the problem. Isolating yourself hasn't done you any good. Come to dinner. Meet everyone. Tony and I will be right there with you in case something happens, but I don't think it will."

It was going to be overwhelming. Sky was sure of that. Whether or not it would scare him or make him panic, he didn't know, and he wasn't sure he wanted to find out—that he could risk it.

Tony reached out from his spot on the couch and grabbed Sky's shoulder. His touch was cool and relaxing, and Sky allowed himself to lean against Tony's leg. He was sitting on the floor between the couch and the coffee table, but Cora and Tony had refused to sit further away from him, and he was glad they had now.

"You need people," Tony said. "You were in that lab for almost a year. You were alone for all that time, and no, the scientists and the guards don't count as company. You're trying so hard to make yourself harmless for people, but you're not allowing yourself to *meet* people. I think part of your problem is precisely that. You need something more concrete to focus on than the idea of not hurting people you don't know. You need to be social. We all do, even the most introverted of us."

"I'm not going to win this argument, am I?" Sky asked.

Cora pointed at him. "This is part of your training."

"No, it's not."

"I'm the coach here. If I say it is, then it is. You're coming to dinner with us. You're not going to set anything on fire."

Sky knew he could refuse, and they'd eventually leave him alone, but they were right. He was lonely, even with Ulric hanging around more often than was healthy for him. "All right. I'm coming to dinner."

Ulric was throwing peas at Armand's head when the stair door opened. He looked up, thinking it was Rocco or the twins since they were late for dinner, but it wasn't. Instead, Cora strode in, followed by Tony and Sky. Ulric froze, and a blob of mashed potatoes hit his forehead.

"That food is for eating, not to paint the walls," Graham grumbled. "I didn't spend the afternoon cooking for you to throw my food around."

"And I hope you know you're going to have to clean the walls if you get them dirty," Win added.

Ulric grabbed his napkin and cleaned his face, but he suspected Sky had already seen him. He looked like he was trying not to laugh, and Ulric rose from his chair to meet him once he thought he was clean.

"This is a surprise," he murmured when he got to his mate.

Sky rubbed the back of his neck. "Cora insisted."

"And she doesn't take no for an answer. I know."

"I tried to make her see this was a bad idea, but like you said, she ignored me."

"I don't think it's a bad idea." But Sky did. That much was obvious by the way he was behaving.

He was looking around, wary as he took in the many people sitting around the table. Ulric wasn't sure why Sky looked so worried, whether it was because of his ability or because almost all the assassins and their mates were there tonight. It didn't often happen, since at least a few of them were always out on jobs, but with the raid to the lab having taken place only a few days ago, they were still going over all the files and testimonies the enforcers had gotten from the scientists. The enforcers usually did all this stuff, but on this occasion, it was close to the assassins' hearts, and they all wanted to do their part.

"Are you sure he's your mate, Ulric?" Armand asked as he too got up from his chair.

Ulric glared at him. He wished he could kill him with his gaze, but unfortunately, he didn't have that ability. "Of course I'm sure."

"Yeah? Because he's way too pretty for you, and probably too nice, too."

He strode toward them, a smile on his face. Armand didn't mean anything with his words, and he wouldn't hurt Sky, but Sky didn't know that. He'd never met Armand before, and Armand could be intimidating at first sight. He had a lot of tattoos and piercings, so even though he was little more than an overgrown puppy, he looked like a biker, and like the assassin he was.

"I'm Armand," he said to Sky, offering his hand.

Sky looked at it as if it were a particularly big spider. He didn't reach for it. Instead, he nodded at Armand. "I'm Sky. I don't mean to be rude, but—"

"That's fine. Not everyone likes shaking hands." Armand dropped his hand, but he didn't go back to his chair. "I was starting to think that Ulric had made you up."

Sky looked around, but there was no escaping Armand. "No, he hasn't. I just needed to get used to this place."

He was trying to hide his ability. Ulric understood why, but he didn't need to. Everyone would be accepting of it here. Sky didn't know that, though, at least not yet, or maybe he didn't believe it.

Ulric cleared his throat. "Why don't you go back to your dinner, or at least the dinner you haven't thrown in my face yet," he snapped.

He didn't mean to be rude, but he knew Armand. He'd want to stick with Sky the entire evening, asking questions and prodding until Sky answered them. Sky would be overwhelmed, and he might start panicking. If there was one thing

Ulric had learned about Sky in the near week since they'd met each other, it was that Sky put a lot of responsibilities on his shoulders. If something happened and he caught fire, he'd blame himself, even if wasn't his fault.

Ulric gently pressed a hand against the small of Sky's back. He steered Sky toward the end of the enormous table that was closest to the door. He gave Dasha an apologetic smile, since he needed to leave his place to Sky, but Dasha didn't seem to notice. He was lost in his thoughts, and he hadn't stopped frowning since he'd come down for dinner. Ulric wanted to know what had happened, and he would have asked if Sky hadn't come up tonight. But now it would have to wait, because Sky was the center of Ulric's attention, as he should be.

"He didn't have to move," Sky said as he watched Dasha sit in the chair Ulric had vacated.

"I'm sure he didn't mind."

"I could have sat in any other free chair."

"Maybe so, but I know you'll be more comfortable with this one."

Sky cocked his head. "Why do you think that?"

"Because it's the one closest to the door. That way, if you feel overwhelmed or think you're about to get *hotter*, you can leave. No one will think ill of you for doing so."

Sky looked like he wasn't sure how to answer to that, so Ulric left him in his chair and went to get a plate. Graham had already gotten there—he took his job of feeding everyone in the house seriously—and he thrust a plate with way too much food on it into Ulric's hands. "You could have told me he was coming for dinner."

"I would have if I'd known." He would have to thank Cora for Sky's presence tonight.

He hadn't expected this to happen for at least another month, if not more. With the way Sky had freaked out when Ulric had told him he wanted to move into the fireproof suite with him, he thought Sky would isolate himself until he had his ability a hundred percent under control.

That didn't seem to be the case, though. It had taken even the best of them a couple of months to be in complete control of their ability, and Sky had been having problems. The fact that his ability was connected to his emotions made every-thing more complicated, especially in this situation.

Ulric kissed Graham's cheek to thank him, ignored Win's glare, and headed back to Sky, who looked out of place and confused. He paused behind Dasha and leaned down so only Dasha would hear him. "Everything okay?" he asked.

Dasha jerked. "What?"

"I wanted to know if everything was okay. You look wor-ried."

Dasha shrugged. "I'm okay. Just tired."

Ulric wouldn't have believed that even if Dasha had been a good liar, and he wasn't. Something was worrying him, and he wasn't able to hide it. As far as Ulric knew Dasha hadn't told anyone about it. Ulric was going to have to push until he got answers, but not now.

He squeezed Dasha's shoulder. "I'm here if you need to talk."

He didn't have to add anything, because Dasha knew. They all did.

"There are a lot of you," Sky said when Ulric reached him.

"There were a lot of us to begin with. But with the mates, we've almost doubled in size."

"Who are the mates? Not to be rude, but at least you guys can defend yourself against me. They can't."

Ulric placed the plate in front of Sky. "Stop worrying. I promise that nothing is going to happen, and even if you do catch fire, no one will be offended by it. We know."

Sky scoffed. "You know what? None of you but Cora know how it feels to not be in control. You have no idea what it feels like to know you could destroy the entire house if you got angry. At least in the fireproof bedroom, I can relax because even if I catch fire, the only things that are going to burn are the ones inside the bedroom. But this place would go down so fast if something happened that I can't help but wonder if I should go back downstairs."

Ulric's heart hurt. He wanted Sky to feel comfortable here, to get to know his family and to become part of it. He'd known it wasn't going to happen anytime soon, but Sky had to start somewhere, and dinner was about as simple as it got. "I know it's overwhelming. I know there are a lot of us, and this is a new place for you and that you're still struggling with your ability. But you're not going to get better if you don't push yourself."

Sky glared. "Why do I like you again?"

Ulric couldn't help but smile. "So you like me? I wasn't sure."

"Of course I like you. You're nice. Everyone here is. That's why I don't want you to get hurt."

That wasn't what Ulric had meant, but it was enough for now.

It was overwhelming. Sky had known it would be, but it didn't help. At least he had Ulric, which was more than he'd expected. He'd been aware that Ulric would be there, and that he would stick by him, of course, but it was touching. Ulric was so eager that he made Sky feel guilty for not allowing him to move into the suite with him. The fact that he'd wanted him there didn't help.

Sky had never liked being alone. He didn't like crowds, and this was getting too close to it for his comfort, but he could deal with it. These people were Ulric and Cora's family, and since he wasn't going anywhere anytime soon, he needed to get used to them. He wished he could have met them little by little, though. Not only were too many people overwhelming and confusing, but their presence terrified Sky. What if something happened? What if for whatever reason he got scared, freaked out, and hurt these people?

"Stop worrying so much," Ulric said, leaning closer.

He'd gotten his plate from where he'd been sitting before and had settled next to Sky. Sky was slightly surprised everyone else had left him alone, nodding at him and smiling but not trying to talk to him. He was curious about them, and he could imagine they were curious about him. But so far, only Ulric and his tattooed friend had tried to get closer.

It was a relief.

"I can't stop worrying," Sky murmured.

"Yeah, you can. And by the way, the thing about none of us understanding what you're going through? That's bullshit."

Sky jerked. "What are you talking about? Cora is the only one—"

"Who can catch fire. Yes, I know. She's also the only other demon here, but that doesn't mean we haven't been through something similar. Didn't I already tell you all of us had been through what you've been through?"

He had, but Sky had thought he was saying it to reassure him. "I didn't know you were serious."

"Of course I was. Look around the table. Most of us here came from a lab. We were all kidnapped or sold by people we trusted. We all spent time being experimented on, like guinea pigs. None of us came out of them the way we went in. That's why we're here. We all have abilities we didn't have before that make us dangerous."

There were like Sky. Sky hadn't thought much about it until now. He'd kept his focus on his own problems. But Cora was a demon, and she shared Sky's ability. Tony's ability was different, but just as strong.

Sky leaned closer to Ulric. "Tell me. Please."

"Only if you eat your dinner."

Sky rolled his eyes, but he obeyed. He was hungry, and being able to eat with other people surrounding him helped. He stuck a forkful of mashed potatoes into his mouth and pointedly looked at Ulric.

Ulric chuckled, and he finally explained, "I'm a wolf shifter. That hasn't changed, but I came out of the lab I was in with the ability to be super-fast."

"How fast is fast?" Because Ulric wouldn't be here if he were only a *bit* faster than most people.

"Very fast. Think airplane past. Or something similar, I guess. I never checked how fast I can go."

"What about the others? Or can you not tell me?"

"I can tell you. It's not a secret. All of us here know what the others can do, even the mates." He pointed his fork at Armand. "He's a unique kind of shifter. He started as human, and now, he can *literally* become other human beings."

Sky blinked. He wasn't sure he'd understood that right. "You mean he could become me if he wanted to?"

"Exactly. He's okay now, but his ability gave him a lot of problems understanding himself and who he was. His mate helped a lot." The fork moved to the man sitting next to Armand. "That's his mate, Beck. He's a mountain lion shifter, and he's not an assassin. He's our IT guy. He's the one who takes care of computers and electronics. He neutralized the security system in the elevators when we raided your lab."

This was fascinating. When Sky had been in the lab, he'd never thought they were people like him out there. He couldn't imagine there would be. What had been done to him was so cruel and unusual, he'd thought he was one of a kind.

And finding out he wasn't was a relief.

"You already know what Tony and Cora can do. Tony's

also a werewolf, and while Cora has always been a demon, she now has extended abilities, just like you. The woman she's sitting next to is a Wendigo shifter. Her name is Heloise, and her ability is empathy. That's why she keeps sneaking glances at you. She can probably feel how worried you are. She and Cora are together, although they're not mates as far as I know."

"Cora didn't tell me about her." Sky wasn't offended. He, Cora, and Tony had mostly talked about his ability and how they could control it. They were friends, but it was going to take some time to get to know each other.

Ulric shrugged. "It's not a secret or anything. Maybe she thought you wouldn't like that? I mean, I told you we were mates, but I never actually asked if you were gay, or sexual, or—"

Ulric was panicking. Sky didn't need to have Eloise's empath ability to know that. He took Ulric's free hand and squeezed. "I'm gay."

Ulric's shoulders slumped. "Good. I mean, I would have been fine even if you'd been straight."

Sky snorted. "That's bullshit too."

Ulric smiled, and while he was gorgeous even when he was scowling, he was even more so with a smile on his face. It made him look younger as if a weight had lifted from his shoulders. "You're right. It is. But I wouldn't have pushed."

"I know. What about the others?" Sky asked. He wasn't ready to talk about his relationship with Ulric. One day soon, he hoped, but not yet.

"Roark is the guy in charge, along with Win. He manipulates minds and makes you think you're somewhere you're not. Win's only supernatural ability is that he can keep all of us in line." Ulric chuckled. "Trust me. He's the only one who can do that. His mate Graham is the cook, and human. Roark is with Noel, who is a human lawyer and helps shifters."

Listening to Ulric talking was oddly soothing. Sky hadn't even realized it, but he'd been relaxing as he listened, and now, he was able to eat without feeling like the food just settled in his stomach like a brick.

"North is a porcupine shifter, and he can make those pointy thingies of his shoot through the skin of his human back. It's pretty creepy. His mate, Milo, is a human and works with Noel. Then there are Evan and Gregory. Don't let their aspect fool you because Evan is the assassin between them. He's a chameleon shifter and can use his animal's ability even when he's human. I know you've already met Lawrence, who's with Griffith. Griffith's father was in charge of the lab we found you in, but he's nothing like that man. Lawrence is a snake shifter, and he's venomous even in his human form, so make sure he doesn't bite you."

Sky probably looked alarmed, because Ulric added, "It's not like he goes around biting people, don't worry. And since he's met his mate, they've been working on controlling the venom in his body. Griffith's some kind of scientist, so he knows what he's doing. But not all of us have our ability under control, and even the ones who do sometimes slip up. You should have been there Cora set the kitchen on fire."

Sky's jaw dropped. "She did *what*?"

"She got angry with someone, I can't remember who it was, but probably Armand. He enjoys pissing people off. But anyway, she lost control for a second and set the kitchen on fire. We're lucky Graham wasn't here yet. He would've kicked our asses."

Sky leaned back in his chair. The food was great, he was surrounded by people, and the conversation he was having with Ulric was fascinating. He hadn't even realized he needed all these things when he'd isolated himself downstairs. He'd been alone a long time in the lab, almost a year from what Rocco had said. Maybe Cora and Tony were right, and he needed people.

"That's Dasha. He's a Nix, but even though he's one of us, he doesn't have other abilities. Miles, on the other hand, can manipulate his body parts. It's all kinds of freaky."

Sky listened to Ulric going on and on about his friends and what they could do. It was evident from his expression and his tone that he loved all of them, and that gave Sky pause. Maybe he'd managed to find a place where he belonged even though he was a freak now. He hadn't allowed himself to hope it would happen, but these people really knew what he had been through, and what he was still going through.

They didn't care

Ulric suspected Sky was overwhelmed by all the information he was spewing, but for some reason, he couldn't seem to be able to shut up.

He was nervous. He wasn't used to feeling nervous when it came guys. He wasn't a Casanova, but he'd had his fair share of one-night stands and relationships. But right now, he might as well be a virgin who didn't know what love was.

He knew it was because Sky was his mate. He wanted to make a good impression, for Sky to like him, and it made him feel like a kid. Maybe he should slip Sky a note and ask him if he liked him, *yes or no*?

"Madison is human and has night vision. She doesn't usually go out on her own. And there's also Frazer, but he's not here today. He's human and controls electricity, just like that little yellow animal from the cartoon." He really couldn't shut up, could he?

At least Sky didn't look bothered. If anything, Ulric suspected he was amused. It was a significant change from how worried Sky had been when he'd first walked in.

Sky swallowed his mouthful of food. "And all of you are

professional killers? Well, except the mates, of course."

"Pretty much. Roark was an assassin, but he's retired, and so is Rocco. The twin Nix, who work with him, aren't assassins though, and neither is Payne."

"Payne?"

"He's probably in his room. He's studying for something or other, and he hasn't been spending a lot of time with the rest of us. He and Gregory used to be slaves to human assholes. Armand rescued them, and he feels a bit like their father, so I'd steer clear of them unless you want him to annoy you to death."

"And here I thought I could start having parties with the bunch of you."

Ulric barked out a laugh. "I just meant that since you came out tonight and that you probably are going to come to dinner often now, you should steer clear of Armand. He doesn't have a mouth-brain filter, so he says pretty much anything that passes through his mind, and that includes questions you probably don't want to answer and things you don't want to know."

"Noted. I'll stay away from him. I find him kind of intimidating."

"He won't hurt you. He's like a big kid in a man's body. I promise. The tattoos and piercings are there to remind him who he is. Nothing more. He's not part of a gang or anything, unless you consider the rest of us as a gang."

Ulric needed to stop talking, dammit. This was getting ridiculous, and he didn't want Sky to think he was an idiot. Although with everything he'd said, maybe it was too late for that.

They listened to the chatter around them for a bit, and even though Ulric wanted to keep on talking to Sky, he didn't want to overwhelm him again. He hoped they'd have more time to talk in the future. Hopefully, Sky was starting to realize that his presence wasn't going to put anyone in danger, and he'd start spending more time with them. Learning control over his ability would also help, and Ulric wished he could do more.

He knew Sky had had enough by the time people started rising from their chairs. He would usually stick around and help clean up, but he hoped no one would mind if he disappeared with Sky. The evening had been a lot for Sky, and Ulric didn't doubt he wanted to retire to his bedroom and have a bit of quiet.

"I'll walk you to your room."

Sky blinked up at him. "I live downstairs. I don't even have to leave the building to get to my bedroom. I can find my way on my own."

"I know. I'd like to walk with you, though." He held his breath until Sky nodded, then said, "Ready when you are."

He got up and looked around. Everyone was ignoring him, and Ulric was pretty sure it was on purpose. God, he loved his family. They knew being in the spotlight would make Sky uncomfortable, and they were making sure it didn't happen.

"Come on. We should leave before they demand we help clean."

"Not helping would make us assholes."

Ulric shook his head. "No one here expects you to hang around any longer that you already have. There were happy to see you, and I'm sure they can't wait for you to come back, but they understand. I told you they do. Hell, Evan barely ever came to dinner before he and Gregory got together and we got rid of that asshole blackmailing him."

"I feel there's a story there."

"There is, but you'll have to ask Evan about it."

"Maybe I will."

Ulric hoped that meant Sky was feeling more comfortable now that he'd seen no one was out to hate him.

They snuck out of the room without anyone saying anything, even though Ulric knew they'd all noticed. He wasn't sure what to say now that he and Sky were alone. He didn't want to start babbling again, so he kept his mouth shut.

Sky didn't say anything else until they reached the door of his suite. When he opened it, he waved Ulric in, but Ulric stayed in the hallway. Sky frowned, and his beautiful smile disappeared. Ulric wanted it to come back, but he wasn't sure how to make that happen. "I want to come in, trust me," he said.

"Why don't you, then?"

"I know that you want me to right now. I'm honored. But I can't help but wonder if it wouldn't be too much and if it's what you want."

Sky's frown deepened. "Why don't you tell me what you think I want?"

Ulric didn't want to make Sky angry, but Sky had asked. "You're feeling good right now. You finally left your rooms, and you realized you're not putting everyone in danger by doing so. You spent time with people. You were overwhelmed, and you probably still are."

"So you're saying I don't know what I want right now?"

"I wouldn't dare. What I mean is that I don't want to overwhelm you even more than you already are."

"I wouldn't have asked if I didn't think I could stand it."

Ulric wasn't sure pushing was the best thing to do in this situation, but maybe Sky needed that. He reached out and carefully cupped one of Sky's cheeks. Sky's breath hitched, but he didn't move away, and he didn't catch fire, which was positive.

Maybe it was pushing too hard, too fast, but Ulric took a step closer. He and Sky didn't quite touch each other except for Sky's cheek and Ulric's hand, but they were close enough for Ulric to feel Sky's warmth. "I want to come in," Ulric murmured. "I want to spread you out on your bed and strip you naked. I want to lose myself in you and for you to lose yourself in me. I want for us to bond, to be one with you, to be able to feel what you feel. I want to be the one you run to when you're in trouble and you need help. But I understand I'm asking too much, too soon."

"Are you asking, though?" Sky croaked.

"I guess I'm asking if you think you can give me a chance. If all of that had a chance to become a reality."

Sky answered, but not with words. Instead, he jerked his arms up, wrapping them around Ulric's neck, and pulled Ulric closer. Their lips locked together as if they've been kissing for decades, and Ulric stopped resisting. He hooked his arms around Sky's waist and pulled him even closer, pressing their fronts together. Sky groaned and opened his mouth.

Then he caught fire.

Ulric felt the warmth before the pain. Sky jumped away before he could seriously hurt Ulric, but he looked horrified. "I'm sorry. God, I'm so sorry."

Ulric raised his hands. "Nothing happened."

"How can you say that? I almost set your head on fire."

He had. The back of Ulric's neck prickled with pain. He schooled his expression so that Sky wouldn't realize that. "I'm okay, I promise."

"I lost control. I could have burned you to a crisp."

"But you didn't, and you're not on fire right now. Your emotions got wild, and yes, you caught fire, but you managed to put the fire out."

Sky looked at his hands as if he hadn't realized that. Ulric hoped it would be enough for him to relax, but it wasn't. Sky shook his head and stepped back, and before Ulric could do anything, he slammed the door in Ulric's face. "You should leave," he said from behind the door.

Ulric sighed. Sky had been doing so well. He knew he

shouldn't have pushed, and he hoped that the step back Sky had just taken wouldn't be impossible to recover from.

CHAPTER FOUR

Sky was *not* opening the door. He knew who was out there, and he wasn't risking it. Ulric had already knocked a few times and asked Sky to let him in, but Sky wasn't about to do that. He might end up setting Ulric on fire, and he would never forgive himself for that. He wasn't sure he could forgive himself for what had happened last night, and that hadn't been that bad.

He'd burned Ulric. He knew it, even though Ulric had told him nothing had happened. But something *had* happened. Sky's hands had caught fire, and he'd burned Ulric. No matter how superficial the burns were, there was no denying that, or the fact that Sky was dangerous.

He should have known better. He should never have agreed to come here. He'd known he was dangerous, but he'd let himself hope he could work things out. Last night was proof he couldn't.

A bang on the door made him jump. He glared, but of course, the person in the hallway couldn't see him.

"Sky? It's Cora."

Sky breathed in and out. He wanted to see Cora. He wanted her to understand he couldn't do this anymore. She'd know what to do. *Right?*

"Sky? What happened? What's going on?"

She wasn't going to leave, was she? Sky might have only met her recently, but he already knew she was stubborn, and that nothing he could do or say would keep her way. He might as well open the door, but he needed to make sure Ulric wasn't going to try to sneak in.

He rose from the couch and shuffled to the door. He could hear Cora talking with someone, two someones from the voices. One of them had to be Ulric, and he suspected the other one was Tony. He pressed a hand to the door. "Only you and Tony can come in," he said.

"Sky!" Ulric cried out.

"No. You're not allowed to come in. I mean it. Stay away."

"I'm not going anywhere." There was the sound of shuffle, then Ulric's voice came stronger and louder. "Please let me in. I promise that nothing happened. I'm fine."

"I'm not opening the door until I'm sure you're not going to barge in." It broke Sky's heart a little to do this, but he couldn't risk it. The only reason he would allow Cora and Tony was that they could defend themselves against him. Ulric couldn't, like last night.

"Come on, Ulric," Cora said. "You need to give him time and space."

"He's only going to use those to distance himself from me. You know that."

Ulric was right. No matter how much Sky wanted to see him, the best thing would be to keep as much distance between them as possible. It would be painful since Sky was Ulric's mate, but it would be better than burning Ulric and hurting him.

"He might, but someone needs to go inside and be with him, and it's not going to be you. You have to allow me and Tony to do it."

Sky could almost imagine Ulric's reaction right now. He might throw his hands in the air as he surrendered, or maybe he was glaring at Cora, his arms crossed over his chest as he tried to think of a way to barge in anyway.

Sky needed to see him. He needed to talk to him, and he needed more of those kisses from last night. Those were all were pointless dreams, though. He couldn't have those things because it was dangerous for Ulric. Touching Ulric, kissing him and thinking about him, made Sky emotional. There were no two ways about it. And Sky being emotional was danger-ous, as last night had shown.

"Sky. I'll stay here. For now," Sky heard Ulric say.

He was relieved as much as he was dismayed. He wanted Ulric to come in. He wanted to talk to him—to see him. He also wanted him to go upstairs so he wouldn't have to know he was out there waiting for him. He needed Ulric to take away the temptation, but he knew better than to think Ulric would do it. Sky was his mate, and he wasn't going to give up without a fight, even if he had to have that fight with Sky.

"Sky? You heard him?" Cora asked.

Sky took a deep breath and reached for the door. He un-locked it and opened it, ignoring Ulric and focusing on Cora and Tony. "Only the two of you," he said again.

He was surprised Ulric didn't try to force his way in, alt-hough he wasn't sure why. Ulric would never force himself on Sky. That much, Sky knew.

Sky stared straight ahead as Cora and Tony walked in, then closed the door and locked it. He turned and pressed his back against it, even though it hurt to be so close to Ulric without being able to see him. When had Ulric become so important to Sky? He shouldn't be. They hadn't had the time to fall in love.

But he'd been there for Sky last night. He'd taken care of him. He'd made sure Sky wasn't overwhelmed, he'd kept his friends at bay, and when Sky had had enough, he'd walked him to his room.

And Sky had almost set him on fire.

Sky wasn't a romantic, but he doubted there was a way to come back from that kind of first date.

Cora put her hands on her hips. "Are you going to tell us

what happened? You were okay last night, but now you're freaking out, and I want to know why."

Sky sighed and rubbed his face. He didn't want to tell Cora and Tony what had happened. It was private. It was also a sign that he was more dangerous than they wanted to admit, though, and they needed to know, even if they ended up kicking him out. Maybe he should leave and make things easier on everyone.

Where would he go, though? He needed to find a place where not a lot of people lived, where he couldn't do damage. He needed to isolate himself, become a hermit. Maybe he could find a cave somewhere.

Cora slapped her hands together right in front of Sky's nose. He jerked and jumped away from the door, blinking at her. "What are you doing?" he asked.

"Bringing you back to reality. You're getting lost in your thoughts, and that's never a good thing."

"Thinking isn't a good thing now?"

"Not in your case. You overthink everything, including trying to control your ability. Now tell us what happened before I open the door and demand answers from Ulric."

She'd do it, which was one of the reasons Sky broke down. "Ulric walked me to my door last night." He shuffled to the couch. He hadn't changed this morning, so he was still in his pajamas, but he didn't care and flopped on the couch, wrapping himself into a blanket.

"We already knew that. It doesn't explain what happened to you."

"He kissed me."

Sky wasn't sure what kind of reaction he'd expected from Cora, but it wasn't her slapping her hands together delightedly. "It's about time. I thought he would kiss you on your first day here."

Sky glared at her. "It's not a good thing."

"Your mate kissing you isn't a good thing?"

"Not when I almost set him on fire because of it."

Cora grimaced. "I see. That would make things harder. I should have realized that's what happened. Ulric kissed you. You got emotional. You caught fire."

"And I kicked him out."

"And now you're worried about hurting him, so you won't let him in again."

"Exactly."

Tony cleared his throat. "You know, what we told you last night is still valid. You need people. You need to have *contact* with people. Even if you do manage to learn to control your ability here on your own, that's all going to go out the window once you have to face people. It's nice and easy to learn control when you're alone, but human beings are going to make you feel emotional one way or another."

"Then maybe I should move away from human beings."

Tony blinked. "What do you mean by that?"

"Just what I said. Since it's obvious I'm not getting any better controlling my ability, maybe I should move to a place where there are no other human beings. That way, I can't hurt them."

"There are people everywhere on this planet."

"Not true. I was thinking of Alaska, but okay, let's say you're right and I can't escape people. Maybe I should kill myself."

Cora sucked in a breath. "What are you talking about?"

"It would be safer for everyone, wouldn't it? I wouldn't be a danger anymore. I'm not sure I'm brave enough to do it, but give me enough time, and I can probably build up to it."

Sky wasn't sure he was serious, but it was an option to consider. He *had* to consider it, for everyone's sake.

Ulric couldn't listen for one more second without intervening. Hearing Sky talking about dying, about killing himself, wasn't something Ulric could ignore.

He slammed up against the door, but the damn thing didn't even budge. He heard Sky cry out, and Cora yelled, "What the fuck are you doing, Ulric?"

"I thought that was obvious," Ulric answered before slamming against the door a second time.

He heard footsteps, but he ignored them, just like he ignored Cora yelling at him. He stepped back, faced the door, and ran at it again. He almost slammed against it, but it opened before he could touch it. So, instead of banging against the door, he ran into the room, and almost fell over the couch.

He managed to stop himself, but he ended up folded against the back of the couch, butt up for everyone to see. He heard Tony guffaw, and he flipped him the bird as he straightened.

"You need to keep that kind of position for Sky's eyes, and only his eyes," Cora said. She'd screwed her eyes shut, and she opened one a bit to peek.

Ulric flipped her the bird, too.

Then he turned to Sky. His mate was sitting on the couch, wrapped into a blanket, and he was staring at him with wide eyes. Ulric had to admit this hadn't been the nicest entrance or the most graceful one. It was the last thing he worried about right now, though.

He pointed his finger at Sky. "You are *not* going to kill yourself."

The shock disappeared from Sky's expression, replaced by a scowl. "You can't tell me what to do."

"You sound like a moody teenager."

"You sound like an asshole."

"That's because I am one. Do you really think I'm going to

stand by and watch you kill yourself?"

"It's my decision to make, not yours."

"You're right, it is, but I have something to say if you decide to do this because you're a coward."

Sky jumped up from the couch and almost fell on his face because of the blanket. He pushed it away, dumping it to the floor. "I am *not* a coward."

"Are you sure about that? Because to me, it looks like you don't even want to make an effort to try to control your ability. You've been here a week, and you're already giving up."

"I'm trying to protect you!"

"I don't need you to protect me!"

Cora leaned over the couch and managed to slap both of them upside the back of the head. Sky jerked back, shock in his expression, but Ulric was used to it. He limited himself to glaring at Cora, but Cora didn't care. She never did. "Stop it, both of you," she spat out.

"He wants to kill himself!" Ulric yelled.

"Do you think we're going to allow him to do that? Stop *yelling*."

"You can't stop me from doing anything," Sky protested.

Cora pointed at him. "I *can* stop you from doing anything I want if I think you're being stupid, and you won't like it if I do, so don't push me. Stop talking about committing suicide and think."

Sky flopped back onto the couch and buried his face into his hands. "I could have killed him," he murmured, just loud enough that Ulric could hear him.

Ulric's heart squeezed. He knew Sky was only thinking about this because he wanted to keep people safe, but that didn't change the fact that it was the wrong thing to do. He couldn't allow Sky to kill himself, even if it was to protect humanity. There had to be another way. He had to *find* another way because he couldn't imagine his life without Sky. It didn't matter how long they'd known each other, or that Sky was pushing him away. Even if Sky never talked to him again, Ulric didn't want a world without him in it.

He tried to keep his tone calm. "You can't give up. You've only been learning for a week. None of us learned control in a week."

Sky's headed jerked toward Ulric. "Your ability isn't dangerous. You don't kill people with it. What happened when you didn't have control over it? You slammed against a wall because you were too fast? I set people on fire, Ulric. I set *you* on fire."

Ulric took a chance and carefully sat next to Sky. He didn't touch him because he didn't think Sky would appreciate it. "You have to give yourself a chance to learn. It was easier for me because I had to understand how to control my shift as a kid. You were human, though. You have no idea how to do this, and a week isn't going to do anything. Besides, you've been doing well."

Sky made a strangled noise. "How can you call burning you doing well?"

"But it was me, Sky. Can't you see it? The reason you caught fire last night is that I was kissing you. Nothing happened at dinner. Your emotions got out of control because I'm your mate. The bond between us is already strong, and I hope you'll always feel strongly when it comes to me."

"You *want* me to set you on fire?"

"Of course not. I like my skin where it is, thank you very much. But it's going to be easier for you to be able to control yourself with people who aren't me." Ulric didn't like that, but he was ready to do just about anything to keep Sky safe. "I could leave the house."

Sky frowned. "What do you mean?"

"I can ask Win to send me on a mission, possibly a long one. I could be away from the house for weeks, maybe a month. That would help you, right?"

"I don't want you to have to leave your home because of me."

"And I don't want you to kill yourself because of me."

Okay, Sky didn't like the thought of Ulric going on a mission. What was left? He needed to learn control around Ulric, and Ulric wanted to keep him safe, but how was he supposed to do that when he wouldn't let Ulric come anywhere near him?

Ulric leaned back against the couch and looked at Cora. "The control he needs to learn. Is it the same one I had to learn for my ability?"

"I suppose it is, or that it's similar anyway. You had to learn how to move slow, to control the speed. He has to control the fire."

"Yes." And it hadn't been easy. Once the scientists were done with Ulric, they hadn't been able to help him. He'd been fast, faster than anyone else in the world. He'd had to re-learn to move, because when he did, it was always too fast, and he ended up scaring people and himself. It was second nature to him now, but in the beginning, it hadn't been. He'd had to focus on it and be conscious of every single movement he made.

"Well, Sky has to be conscious of the power inside him. I'm sure that if he had focused on it last night, he would have been able to feel the moment his ability got out of control. He would have been able to stop it before you got hurt."

"I didn't get hurt." Ulric needed Sky to know that.

"Yeah, you did. Do you think I'm stupid? I'm sure you ran straight to Rocco and his Nix healers so that I wouldn't see the burn on your neck."

Ulric had. He wasn't about to admit it, though, not when Sky was still so freaked out about it. "Okay, so you're worried about staying here because you don't want to hurt the other people who live here, right?"

Sky nodded. "I'm a danger. I don't know how any of you can deny that."

"We're not denying you *could* be a danger. That's why you need to learn to control your ability. It's obvious I'm the biggest hurdle, so I have an idea."

Sky wrinkled his nose. "Why you do I feel like I'm not going to like it?"

"Probably because you won't. But hear me out. You obviously have some control over yourself now. You went to dinner last night, and nothing happened. You didn't start smoking or anything."

"I don't start smoking. I catch fire."

"Whatever. What I'm trying to say is that it looks like you *do* have control around most people by now. Tony and Cora never got hurt while working with you. The only person you have a problem with is me."

"Where are you going with this?"

"I want you to learn to control yourself around me. You're my mate. Even though it feels hopeless right now, I'm not going anywhere, and I'm planning to have decades with you. You don't want to risk putting anyone else in danger, and I get that. But you need to learn control around me. I can teach you that. Maybe not as well as Cora, but I can."

Sky moved back, putting more distance between himself and Ulric. "I don't want to hurt you."

"You might. You have to face that, just like you have to face the fact that I'm willing to put myself in danger so that you can learn control. I want to, because I want to have a future with you. So I think we should find an isolated place where we can stay, maybe with a tent or something. That way you won't hurt anyone but me. I'll take my phone with me so I can call Dasha if I need him to come and heal me. He can be there in seconds. We'll stay together, alone in the middle of the forest or wherever you want to go until you can touch me and kiss me without setting anything on fire."

Sky hadn't heard that correctly, right? He couldn't have. There was no way Ulric was suggesting they spend any amount of time together, alone, in the middle of nowhere. "You're nuts."

Ulric seemed to think it was the best idea ever, though. "It makes sense. You know how to control yourself around other people, but you don't know how to do it around me. That means that I'm a danger to other people, too."

"That doesn't make sense."

"It does. We can't be together around other people because there is always the danger that you'll catch fire, right? I want you to be happy here if you decide to stay. I want you to consider the others like a family, the way I do. That won't happen if you can't stay."

"Maybe I'd rather not stay." But he did, so much. He wanted to see his family again, of course, but he wasn't human anymore. He didn't even look the way he had when they'd last seen him. Even if he ever managed to have full control over his ability, he didn't think he could fit into his old life again, no matter how much he wanted to — and he didn't. He'd seen things, had gone through so much, and he wasn't the same man anymore. He didn't think he could ever get used to his old life again.

The assassins, Cora and Tony and Ulric, were offering him a new life. He wouldn't have to hide what he was with them. He could be himself without fearing that they'd reject him. They already knew all there was to know about this new him, and they didn't care. They'd welcomed him, even though he was a danger for all of them. He wanted to stay here. But he could only do that if he managed full control.

Ulric was right. Sky wanted to stay, and he couldn't ask Ulric to leave. The assassins were his family much more than they were Sky's. But there was a way for both of them to stay. Sky would have to work, and it wouldn't be easy, but hard work had never scared him. He wasn't even sure why he'd been thinking about killing himself. He'd never do that, not when there was another way. But he'd been scared, and he still was.

"It's too big a risk," he said.

"But it's a risk I'm ready to take. I'm *willing* to take it."

"I wouldn't be able to live with myself if anything happened to you."

Ulric reached for Sky's hand, and even though Sky knew he should have moved away, he didn't. He wanted Ulric's hands on him, in so many ways, but right now, it was for comfort. Sky was terrified and confused, and he had no idea how to push out those emotions. He was surprised he hadn't already set the couch on fire.

"I can't promise nothing will happen to me," Ulric said. "We don't know what the future will be like, and even though I have faith in you, accidents happen all the time. But I *do* have faith in you, and I trust you to do everything you can to avoid that happening. I know you're going to work hard now to have a goal. You're not going to let what the scientists did to you influence the rest of your life, not when it could be a very long one if you bond with me. We'll be careful, and we'll make sure to have Dasha on speed dial, but we need to do this. For you, and me."

Sky was floored by the confidence Ulric had in him. He didn't have it in himself, and he didn't see how Ulric could be so sure Sky would make it.

What were his other options, though? He didn't have ideas. He could spend his time in this fireproof room, isolating himself and living in fear of hurting someone. He could ask Ulric to go on missions so they wouldn't be in the house at the same time.

Or he could accept what Ulric was saying, the possibility that they could work this out, and go with him. "What do you have in mind?" he asked.

Ulric's shoulders slumped. He looked relieved, and Sky knew he'd done the right thing. "I haven't thought about it yet."

Sky laughed. He felt lighter, even with the work that was waiting for him. "I should have known you were suggesting this even though you don't know how to go about it."

"I was trying to make sure you didn't hurt yourself. I was terrified. But now that you're safe, we can put our heads together and make decisions."

Cora cleared her throat. "Not that I'm not happy that Sky finally stopped being an idiot, but you're going to have to clear this with Win."

"That's not going to be a problem, but I want to go to him with a plan already in place."

"Let's do this, then."

Cora and Tony settled on the floor on the other side of the coffee table. Sky blinked at them, awed by the fact that they weren't running away from him. He'd scared the scientists and the guards in the lab, especially after he'd killed one of them. Most of them had wanted nothing to do with him, and they'd only taken him out of his cell when they had to. They hadn't tried to teach him control. They'd only wanted him to kill on command, and he hadn't been willing to compromise on that.

He'd never wanted to be a killer. The guard's death still weighed on him, on his soul, and he wondered if he'd ever get over it. He still had nightmares, and it would only get worse if he hurt anyone else. The only options he had to make sure that didn't happen were to either kill himself or learn to control his ability. He wasn't getting rid of it. Rocco had been clear about that. No matter how little Sky liked being able to set things on fire with a thought, it was what it was. It was *him* now.

And he needed to learn to live with it.

"Where would you go?" Tony asked.

"I don't know. Do you have any suggestions?" Ulric asked.

Tony chuckled. "Trust you not to know. I bet you thought about this solution seconds before you blurted it out."

"You know I did. Now stop teasing me and get to work."

"What about camping?"

"Won't I risk setting the entire forest on fire?" Sky asked. He wasn't willing to kill anyone, but he also wasn't willing to destroy a forest.

"You can pick a place that's in the forest, but not too close to trees. I'm sure there are camping spaces that are isolated enough for you to be safe there but also not close enough to the forest to risk burning to the ground."

"It's going to take a little research," Cora said. "Like Tony said, I'm positive we can find something. What you need is a place where no one is going to bother you, where you can be at least comfortable enough with a tent or something like that, and where nothing will burn down to the ground if you catch fire."

"Doesn't the council own forest space?" Tony asked.

"It docs. I'm not sure where the spaces are, but it would be the best way to be sure no one is going to hike in and surprise Sky. Ulric is going to have to ask Win, but since he needs to talk to him anyway, that shouldn't be a problem. He'll be able to suggest the best place to do this. He wants Sky to succeed as much as we do."

It sounded like they had a plan. Sky had never gone camping, and he had no idea what it would be like, but he'd deal with it. There was no other way for him to do this.

The thought of spending time alone with Ulric was scary, in several ways. Sky hoped he wouldn't hurt Ulric, and he would do everything in his power to make sure it didn't happen. Ulric's presence was enough for him to feel flustered. He didn't know how to process that. He didn't know how to deal with the fact that they were about to become tentmates.

But his feelings about Ulric weren't going to change, and their bond wasn't going to disappear. Sky didn't *want* anything to change. He enjoyed feeling this way, flustered and happy, and he wanted a future with Ulric.

But he couldn't deny that those emotions made everything more complicated.

Ulric had left Sky in his room to pack and to talk to Cora. She wanted to give Sky a few pointers that she hadn't gotten to in the past week. Sky would need all the help he could get to make it through this, and Ulric was happy he wouldn't be the only one helping. He wouldn't have minded, but Sky needed more than just him in his life. Ulric had other things to do right now, though. He knew convincing Win that this was the best option for everyone wouldn't be easy. Win was overprotective of his assassins, but he also knew when to allow them to follow their own minds. Besides, Ulric was going, whatever Win thought of his decision.

Win was in his office with Roark, and Ulric wasn't sure if that was a good thing or not. Roark tended to trust the assassins more because he'd been one himself, but that didn't mean he'd be okay with Ulric's plan, not with the risks it implied.

They both looked up when Ulric knocked on the door. Win waved him in, and Ulric made a beeline for one of the empty chairs on the other side of Win's desk.

"Is Sky okay?" Win asked.

"He's good. He's the reason I'm here, actually."

"He is? We're listening."

Ulric rubbed the back of his neck. "I'm sorry if I'm disturbing you, but this couldn't wait."

"Don't worry about that."

"Sky burned me last night. He didn't mean to, but I kissed him, and his emotions got out of control. He's been talking about killing himself, and that's not something I can allow him to do."

"No one here wants that to happen. What do you have in mind?"

Ulric was relieved that Win was taking this seriously. "I want to take him away."

Win cocked his head. "Away?"

"Yes. I think Sky and I should spend time together . . . alone. It's obvious from last night that he can control his power well enough when he's with other people. He was okay at dinner, and the only moment he slipped was when I was with him. I want to work on that with him."

"You don't need to go way to do that."

Ulric had expected that. "We don't, but he's terrified he's going to hurt someone here. I think his fear is one of the reasons he's having such a hard time controlling his emotions, and as a result, his ability."

"Going God knows where alone with him might make things even harder for both of you."

"It might, but it also might help him more than what Cora and Tony are doing. Look, I wouldn't suggest this if I thought he'd continue learning with them. He *wants* to learn, but the thought of being here and possibly hurting someone is blocking him. Since we know that I'm the biggest reason he loses control, I think we can make it work."

Win didn't look happy, but he still nodded. "What did you have in mind, exactly?"

"Camping. I know it sounds stupid, but if I could get Sky

alone for an extended length of time in the middle of no-where, I think it would help him. We need a place where no one is going to stumble on to us, a place where we can be safe and where he's not going to have to worry about hurting anyone."

"Won't he worry about hurting you?" Roark asked.

"He's terrified at the thought, but he's going to have to get over it. I'm hoping that not having to worry about anyone else will help."

"What if you get hurt?"

"I'll go talk to Rocco before leaving, of course, and I have both him and Dasha on speed dial, just in case." Ulric leaned forward. "I'm doing this willingly. I want to help him. I want a future with him, since he's my mate, and that's not going to happen if he freaks out every time I kiss him."

Win sighed heavily. "What do you need from me?"

Ulric relaxed. Win hadn't said yes, but he also hadn't said no, and Ulric suspected he leaned toward the first answer. "We were talking with Cora and Tony, and one of them suggested using council land. That way we can be sure no one is going to hike up to our tent and surprise us."

"Are you sure you want to go camping for weeks? How are you going to get food?"

"I can hunt if things come to that, but I'm hoping you'll allow Dasha or one of the twins to shimmer to us every so often."

It was a big thing to ask, but Sky was family, since he was Ulric's mate. Ulric hoped it meant something. He *knew* it meant something to Win, but he couldn't be sure Win would think with his heart rather than his brain.

"I don't like this," Win said.

"I know. Trust me. I wouldn't do it if I didn't think it was necessary. But Sky has to get over it, and the fastest and surest way to make it happen is this."

"I'm also not sure your reasoning on this is correct, but since Sky burned you last night, it's obvious his training needs to be more intensive. Are you sure you don't want Cora and Tony to go with you?"

Ulric had thought about it. It would probably be a good idea to have both of them there, but he didn't want them to be. "I'll call them if I feel I need them, but they've already been training with Sky for a week. He knows everything he could learn from them. His only problem now is understanding how to use that knowledge."

"And you think he's going to learn how to use it by camping alone with you in the woods."

It wasn't a question, but Ulric nodded. "But if you have another option . . ."

Win waved Ulric away. "You have my approval on this. Take your phone with you, and make sure to keep it charged. Call if you need anything, and when I say anything, I do mean *anything*. Take everything Rocco suggests with you, and feel free to call Dasha anytime you need him. I'll make sure not to send him on a mission until you and Sky are back." Win rubbed his face. "I hope you're right on this. I want Sky to become part of the family, but if he can't control himself, I don't see how it's going to be possible."

Ulric knew that. If push came to shove, he'd take Sky and leave with him. It would kill him to leave this family behind, but it would be the best thing for Sky, and that meant it would be the best thing for Ulric. Besides, he also had a blood family. Unlike some of the assassins, Ulric's family had welcomed him back when he'd been freed from the lab. They didn't know what he did for a living, since he didn't want to put them in danger, but they wouldn't mind if he suddenly appeared on their porch.

Ulric got up. "Thank you. I don't know what I would have done if you'd said no."

Win chuckled. "You would have done it anyway. I'll send you the coordinates to an empty stretch of land you can use. Stay safe, both of you."

Ulric's next stop was the infirmary. That was where Rocco could be found most days, and today wasn't any different. He was reading some medical magazine, but he put it down when he heard Ulric walk in. His eyebrows rose on his forehead, and he asked, "Is everything okay? I thought you'd already come last night."

Right. Of course Jolyn had told him Ulric had come by. "Jolyn healed me, don't worry. That's not why I'm here. Sky and I are leaving for a bit, and I need you to tell me what to do if he accidentally burns me."

Rocco's eyes widened. "Accidentally burns you?"

"I already cleared this with Win. I know it's probably a stupid idea, but it's the best one I could come up with, and I'm going to do it. Please, I just need you to teach me how to treat burns."

"I don't know why I even bother with you and the others. I heal you, make sure you're healthy, then you throw yourself into danger even though you don't need to." Rocco sounded annoyed, but he still got up and waved at Ulric to follow him. "I'm going to give you a packet with everything you'll need if you happen to get burned, but if the burn is a bad one, I want you to come back here as soon as you can. I'm not kidding, Ulric. I know you want to help Sky, but that's not going to happen if you get a third-degree burn."

"I promise."

And he wasn't lying. Ulric wanted to help Sky, but he knew Sky would be even more afraid than he already was if he hurt Ulric badly. Besides, Ulric was planning to be around for a long time, so letting Sky kill him accidentally was out of the question.

CHAPTER FIVE

Once again, Sky had no idea where he was. At least this time, he wasn't afraid. He trusted Ulric and Dasha, and he knew they'd never put him in danger.

He and Ulric had left the warehouse where the assassins lived. Sky should probably feel guilty about having Ulric leave his home and his family, but he couldn't bring himself to feel that way. He *did* feel guilty about putting Ulric in danger, but there was no way out of that. At least he wouldn't be a danger to everyone else in the house. He hated putting Ulric's life in jeopardy, but he'd already learned that Ulric wouldn't take no for an answer, not when he wanted to hear yes.

Sky dropped his hand from Dasha's shoulder and looked around. The sky wasn't completely dark yet, and he could see Dasha had brought them to a small open space between the trees. Ulric had told him he'd asked Win to use a patch of land the council had available so they could be sure no one was going to stumble onto them. It made Sky feel better, and he was finally beginning to have more faith in the fact that maybe he could do this.

It wasn't going to be easy, but at least he could forget the fear for a bit. The only person whose life was in danger right now was Ulric, but Sky wouldn't have sent him back for anything.

The fact that he and Ulric were mates still amazed him. He could have gone his entire life without meeting Ulric if he'd been human and had still lived with his family, and that fact, too, was hard to wrap his mind around. Knowing that he had to thank the scientists at the lab for something made his stomach churn, but he was looking forward to spending time with Ulric and possibly exploring the bond between them. They hadn't had a chance to do that yet, since they'd both been focused on Sky and his problem at controlling his ability, but maybe now they would.

Dasha wrinkled his nose. "Are you sure you want to stay?"

Ulric dumped his backpack on the ground. "Of course we are. Why?"

"It's a bit . . . empty. Is there even a bathroom here?"

Ulric laughed. "Of course not. We're in the middle of the forest. What did you expect?"

"I don't know. Maybe a trailer or something."

"The point of this is to make sure that Sky doesn't burn anything to the ground."

And with Sky's luck, he'd end up burning the tent, but at least that would be easily replaceable. What wouldn't be replaceable was Ulric, but Sky had promised himself he'd work as hard as he had to to make sure nothing happened to his mate. He'd already burned him once, and he wouldn't let that happen twice, even though Ulric had tried to convince him he didn't mind. Who wouldn't mind getting burned on a regular basis?

That meant no physical contact and no more kisses until Sky was sure he wouldn't catch fire, and that was a torture in itself. Now that he knew what kissing Ulric was like, he wanted more kisses and everything that came with being mates. He couldn't believe how close he felt to Ulric considering how little they'd talked and how little time they'd known each other. But that was the mate bond, right? It was supposed to work like this. It was supposed to make them both feel like they wanted to be together.

When he'd been human, Sky had wondered if he'd ever

find out he was someone's mate. He hadn't been sure what to think about it. On the one hand, it felt romantic. Being bonded to someone for the rest of your life, knowing they were it for you and that you were it for them, all of that felt a bit like a romance novel. On the other hand, Sky hadn't been sure what to think about a bond influencing him. Would he have been attracted to Ulric even without the bond?

Sky looked at Ulric, who'd started unrolling the tent, or whatever it was he was doing. Sky had never been an outdoorsy person, and he wouldn't have known where to start if Ulric hadn't been here with him.

Yeah, he probably would have been attracted to him anyway. Ulric was a good-looking guy, and Sky would have seen that even if they hadn't been mates. But it was more than that. Ulric was a good person. He was also stubborn, and apparently, once he made a decision, nothing would change his mind about it. He'd known how scared Sky was of hurting the people in the warehouse, and he'd found a solution for it. Sky hoped it wasn't going to end with him getting hurt, but that possibility made him want to work harder.

He'd been doing his best learning from Cora and Tony, but it hadn't been enough. He needed to do more if he wanted to have a chance at a normal life, or at least, as normal as it could be now that he wasn't human anymore.

Looking at himself in the mirror still freaked him out some days. He'd had green eyes when he'd been human, and they were still green, but now the green swirled with black. It gave Sky an otherworldly appearance and made the fact that he wasn't human anymore so visible that he was terrified at the thought of going home to his family. What would they think about him now? Would they accept him, or would they kick him out because he wasn't the Sky they'd known?

They'd accepted he was gay without too many problems, but this was something else entirely. What the scientists had done to him made him not human anymore.

"I could use some help," Ulric called out.

Dasha and Sky looked at each other. "Do you know what he's doing?" Dasha asked.

"No idea."

"Well, I guess you're going to have to find out, because I'm out of here. I have things to do."

Ulric chuckled. "Of course you have things to do. Trust you to run when we need your help setting up the tent."

Dasha glared at him. "I *do* have things to do." His expression softened. "But call me if you need anything, and I do mean anything. Well, as long as it doesn't have anything to do with setting up your tent. I wouldn't know where to start even if you gave me instructions."

"I have my cell phone and your number on speed dial. Don't worry about us. We'll be okay, and eagerly waiting for your return with food in a few days."

"I knew you only wanted me for my food."

Ulric was still laughing when Dasha shimmered away after waving at Sky. Now they were alone, and Sky wasn't sure what to do. He knew he ought to be helping Ulric, but like Dasha, he had no idea where to start. "You're going to have to give me instructions," he said.

Ulric snorted. "Of course I am. Why don't you walk around and get some wood for the fire?"

Sky blinked. "We're going to have a fire? Can we do that without burning down the forest?"

Ulric groaned. "You have no idea how to do this, do you?"

"Hell no. I've never gone camping. I like my comforts." And the thought of doing his business in the woods for God knew how long was terrifying. That was one of the reasons he had to focus on getting this right, and soon. He wanted to go back to his bathroom.

By the time he was back with a small stack of wood, Ulric

had managed to set up the tent. He'd also gathered a bunch of stones from somewhere, and he'd arranged them in a circle by the tent. He'd taken out two folding chairs, and Sky had no idea where he'd gotten them. Had all that stuff already been here, or had Ulric brought it? And if he'd brought it, where had he put it?

"Put the wood in the pit, please," Ulric said. "I brought something to light it."

Sky arched a brow. "Really?"

Ulric frowned. "Of course. How else are we supposed to — oh."

"Yes, oh." Sky crouched next to the pit and put the kindling he'd found into it. He had no idea how people who couldn't do what he could do lit a fire when they didn't have a lighter, but he'd never have to worry about it again—not that he was planning to go camping again once this was over.

Sky swallowed and stared at the wood. He could do this. His main problem with his ability right now was not having control were Ulric was concerned. But Cora had taught him how to light only his hand, or even his finger, on fire, so he could do this.

He focused on his ability and his finger, then set himself on fire.

Watching Sky using his ability made Ulric emotional. He knew how hard Sky had worked to get to this point, to the point where he could set only a finger on fire. He also seemed so relaxed while he was doing it that Ulric was pretty sure it would become second nature in no time. Then Sky wouldn't need him anymore, or rather, he wouldn't need to be isolated with him anymore.

Ulric realized this wasn't why they were there, but he couldn't help but hope that this camping together thing would help them get closer. He knew Sky wouldn't allow himself to do that until he had control of his ability, because he was too scared of hurting him, but Ulric was positive that eventually they'd be able to kiss and hopefully do more without him getting barbecued.

Sky leaned back and stared at the fire. He looked smug, satisfied, and Ulric couldn't help but wonder if that was what he'd look like in bed.

Nope. Ulric needed to stop thinking about that before he drove himself crazy. He wanted Sky in his bed, there was no doubt about that, and he suspected Sky wanted the same. Sky had kept himself at arm's length, but that was only because he was afraid he'd hurt Ulric. He'd been more than eager to kiss Ulric back the other evening, though.

Ulric wanted more of that. Even if they didn't have sex, he wanted to feel closer to Sky. They hadn't known each other long, but both Ulric and his wolf needed Sky.

Ulric cleared his throat. That would only happen if Sky managed to control his ability where Ulric was concerned. Ulric couldn't push him because that wouldn't end well. "That was impressive. Did Cora teach you to do it?"

Sky rose from his crouch. "She did. She taught me to control the amount of power I use and to restrict the fire to only the body part I want to burn."

"In only a week? You've been working hard. I was nowhere near as close as you are in controlling my ability after a week."

Sky settled into the chair next to Ulric's. He seemed hesitant, and Ulric waited, giving him the time he needed to put his thoughts in order. "You told me your ability is that you're fast?" Sky finally asked.

Ulric nodded. "It is."

"Do you want to talk about it? Only if you're okay with it, of course."

Ulric had talked about it more than a few times. He'd been so lost in the beginning, and no one had been able to help him. Back then, every time he moved, it was too fast for people to see him. It had taken a lot of work and self-control for him to get where he was now. Luckily for him, he was a shifter, and he had decades to learn control.

"Everything was weird in the beginning. I was still in the lab, and the scientists wanted me to learn control because, well, they couldn't even see me when I moved. I don't think they got what they wanted from me. I mean, a superfast soldier is useful, of course, but they couldn't get me to stay still for long enough to teach me control. Besides, I doubt they'd have managed. They had no idea what they were dealing with, even though they were the ones who created me."

"That sounds pretty much like what happened to me."

"It is, in a way. Only it took me much longer than a week to learn control."

"But you know it now. I've wondered if the fact that you were moving like me is because you're controlling yourself every second of the day."

Ulric rose from his chair. "You see that purple flower over there, by the trees?"

Sky looked at it, and Ulric moved.

It was always exhilarating to use his ability. Ulric had to be so careful all the time, and it felt like a relief when he could finally let go when he did this. He ran to the flower, picked it up, and ran back to Sky before Sky was even able to say anything. He held it out, and Sky blinked at it. "That's . . ."

"It's the purple flower I asked you about."

Sky took it. "I didn't even have the time to say that I was able to see it."

"I know. That's how fast I am."

"God, I can't imagine how hard it is for you to move at the same pace the rest of us do."

Ulric shrugged and sat back in his chair. "I won't lie, some-times I wish I could say fuck it and let go. But my family is too important to me. I don't want to have to leave them be-hind. Besides, it would be a lonely life if I did. There's no way I could fit in with humans."

"It takes a lot of control, every second of the day, right?"

"It does. It's second nature for me by now, though. It's been years since I learned, and it will be the same for you once you do. I know it feels like it's an insurmountable obstacle right now, but you're young, and it hasn't been that long since you received this ability. I truly believe that you've been doing great."

"Maybe. I wish I was better at it, though."

"Why? You managed to set your finger on fire just now. You had dinner with everyone else last night, and nothing happened."

"Except you. I burned you."

Ulric wasn't surprised that Sky still blamed himself for that. "I went to the infirmary, and I was healed within ten minutes. I promise I wasn't in pain for long. You have to for-give yourself, because I feel like this is going to become yet another obstacle to your control."

"I'm starting to see that."

Sky looked down the flower he was still holding, avoiding Ulric's gaze. "I know I can control myself enough not to be a danger to people, but when you're in the mix, I can't. I don't know why that is or how to change it, and I know it's my problem and not yours, but I have to face that."

Ulric took a chance and gently patted Sky's knee. "Of course it's my problem." Maybe they should talk about this. Sky wanted Ulric as much as Ulric wanted him, but as far as Ulric knew, it might only be physical for him.

Ulric swallowed. This was hard, as hard as learning control had been, albeit in a different way. "What do you want from me?" he asked quietly.

Sky looked up. "What do you mean?"

"Well, it was obvious that you wanted to kiss me as much as I wanted to kiss you."

Sky snorted. "That would be an understatement."

It made Ulric feel a bit better, but it still wasn't answering his question. "Is it only physical, though? I mean, I do want to have sex with you, obviously, but that's only a part of what I want from you."

"You don't pull punches, do you?"

"I could, but I think we need to be honest with each other, considering the situation we're in." Ulric was terrified of what Sky's answer would be, but he had to face it. He always tried to face things, especially when they were hard and when he wanted to run.

Sky sighed. "Since you want me to be honest, I have to tell you that I'm not sure what I want. I mean, it's obvious I want to have sex with you. Even a blind person would. But it's not just physical. I love how you're trying to take care of me, even though you're putting your life in danger to do it. No matter how hard or how many times I pushed you away, you'll always come back, and right now, that makes me feel like you're the only rock in my life. I *am* a little confused about the bond, whether or not I would have found you attractive or if I would have felt the same way I do without it, but I realize it's pointless to think that way. The bond is what it is, and I can't ignore it or wonder what would have been without it."

"So?"

Sky looked straight at Ulric. "I want to learn control so that you can kiss me without burning yourself. I want to not be afraid to touch you when I want to touch you. I can't promise anything beyond that. I won't tell you we have a future together when I'm not sure we do. You might be ready to do everything you can to help me, but I'm ready to do anything

I can to make sure you're okay. Even if it means leaving you behind."

It was frustrating. Sky wished he could tell Ulric he wanted to date him, but he couldn't, not when dating him could be lethal. He couldn't make any promise until he learned absolute control around Ulric.

"I can live with that," Ulric said.

"Are you sure? Because I don't expect anything from you, not the help you've been giving me or for you to hang around and wait for me to be ready." It was hard to say that because Sky *did* want Ulric to stay around. He wanted Ulric to help him, but he realized it might be too much, even for a mate.

Ulric glared. "I'm not going anywhere, whether you like it or not. And I know you were serious when you said you were ready to leave if you don't manage control when you're with me. So now that we've been honest with each other, we can move forward."

"Forward?"

Ulric moved slowly, so Sky knew he was about to take his hand before he did, but it was still startling.

Ulric's skin was cool against Sky's. Sky knew his body temperature had gone up a few degrees since he'd gotten his power, because Rocco had told him. He hadn't been touching a lot of people recently, though, and he hadn't expected the difference to be that obvious.

Ulric chuckled. "You're going to be nice to have in my bed once winter comes."

Sky couldn't help it—he laughed. "Cold feet?"

"Always."

It was nice to imagine a life where they would go to bed together and Sky would get to warm Ulric up. Sky needed to cling to that image. He needed to make sure he remembered why he was doing this, even when it was so hard that he wanted to give up.

Ulric squeezed Sky's hand, and Sky felt a flutter in his stomach. "Why don't you try to set your other hand on fire?" Ulric asked.

So they'd already started. Sky supposed it was a good thing, but he wanted to go back to the easy conversation. He didn't want to train right now, especially not when Ulric was touching him and risking his hand. But this was why they were there, and the sooner he did it, the sooner they could go home.

Sky swallowed and closed his eyes. For now, it was easier for him to control his ability when he wasn't distracted. The sounds of the forest around him were enough to do that, so closing his eyes helped.

It took him a bit longer to set his finger on fire then it had to light the wood in the fire pit, and even then, he couldn't keep the fire to his finger. The flames danced on his hand, and he glared at it when he opened his eyes.

"Okay, that's not exactly a finger, but it's something. Better than I expected," Ulric said. "Now turn it off."

Sky closed his eyes again, but before he could do anything, Ulric's fingers moved on his hand. Ulric stroked Sky's palm, and Sky's groin grew tighter.

His entire arm caught fire.

Sky jerked away. The fire hadn't been on Ulric's side, but he needed to be sure nothing would happen to his mate. He also needed to be far from Ulric to turn the fire off.

Thankfully, Ulric stayed where he was while Sky breathed in and out and tried to calm himself. It was ridiculous. A simple touch of fingers shouldn't make Sky feel like he was about to explode.

It took him way too long to be able to put the fire out. Once he managed, he felt like he'd run a marathon. He wanted to sit in the chair again, but he hesitated — enough that Ulric realized what was happening.

Ulric raised his hands. "I won't touch you again. I promise. Sit down and rest."

Sky flopped down, grateful. "I'm sorry."

"You have nothing to be sorry about. I know it's hard. And I know I made it even harder on you."

"Maybe, but it's what you have to do. I can't be around people or you if I catch fire every time you touch me."

"That *is* going to make it harder for us to have sex."

Ulric's words started Sky into laughing. "You sound convinced it's going to happen."

"That's because it is. I know what you said about leaving me behind if you think is the best for me, but I have hope. I know you can do it, and the more you want to be in my life, the more you work on this."

He wasn't wrong. Sky did want him in his life, and just like he was ready to do anything to keep Ulric safe, he wanted to do everything in his power to have Ulric around.

He wanted everything Ulric was offering. Not only the sex but the love, the bond. Sky wasn't going back to his old life. He had to deal with that thought and to start thinking about the new life he had now. He'd been one of the lucky ones, because he still had a chance at living the way he wanted to.

And now, surprisingly, that included Ulric.

He held a hand out. "I want to try again."

"Are you sure? I know how tired you have to be already."

Sky had to build resistance. Training with Cora had been exhausting, and he'd usually gone to bed right after they were done. But he wasn't going to obtain anything by taking it easy and giving up after the first try. "Again, please."

Ulric took Sky's hand without hesitating. Sky was amazed that Ulric didn't think twice about it. He knew he could get hurt, yet there he was, holding hands and waiting to see if Sky was about to set him on fire.

Sky closed his eyes, and as soon as he had, Ulric's fingers moved on him. He felt Ulric trace his knuckles with his thumb, then slipped a finger between their hands and tickling his palm.

Sky swallowed. He had to stay focused, no matter what Ulric was doing to him.

"Only your finger," Ulric murmured.

Sky could do this.

He hoped.

He could feel the fire inside him building. Ulric's touch was like throwing gasoline onto it. The fire wanted to come out — to consume.

Sky wouldn't let it.

He channeled the fire to his hand, but he knew he'd failed again right away. He could feel the heat coming from his entire arm, and he supposed he should feel lucky that only his arm had caught fire.

He huffed and let go of Ulric's hand. It was slightly easier to put the fire out this time, but he still felt like he'd achieved nothing.

"I know you're frustrated."

Sky turned to face Ulric. "Of course I am. I can't seem to touch you without losing control."

The corner of Ulric's lips curled into a smile. "That's not something I mind."

Sky wanted to slap him, but he liked Ulric's hair and didn't want to burn it. "You know that's not what I meant."

"I do. But you have to realize that even once you manage control, there are moments in which you're going to lose it, especially at the beginning. Can you imagine keeping up the control you use on your ability when you're with Cora while we are in bed together? Maybe as you come?"

Shit. That wasn't something Sky had thought about, and

now he needed to. "Maybe we should never have sex."

Ulric barked out a laugh. "I certainly hope we will, but if you don't wish to, that's okay too. I do hope this gives you something to work toward to."

Sky raked a hand through his hair. "Isn't there an easier way to do this? Or at least to make things easier for me." He hated losing control.

Sky knew there might be something when Ulric hesitated. He wanted to push, but he gave Ulric the time to decide he wanted to talk about this.

"There might be something," Ulric finally said.

"What? I'm ready to do just about anything to happen, and you know that."

"I'm not a hundred percent sure this will work, but I think it might be easier for you to do this if we were bonded."

That wasn't what Sky had expected to hear.

Ulric knew it was too soon. He didn't expect Sky to say yes. Hell, it wasn't like he'd asked Sky if he wanted to bond. Sky had asked a question, and Ulric had answered, that was it. Still, Ulric couldn't help the trepidation he felt as he waited for Sky to digest the news.

Sky slowly nodded. "You think bonding will help? How?"

"Well, I think it will both help and make things harder for you, especially in the beginning. It might be harder because you'll feel what I feel, and it might overwhelm you, but it might also help you understand when you lose control. You'd be able to feel if I'm in pain . . . if I'm worried or scared." Ulric hesitated. He was nowhere sure of this, but it was a possibility, and he wanted Sky to know. "I might also be able to guide you through the bond. You could feel how calm I am and how I do things when I control myself, and I hope it will help you."

Sky wrinkled his nose. "It's not a certainty, though, right?"

"Nothing is when it comes to us. It's not like there are other shifters like us out there, except for Cora, of course. But no one can help because this isn't a situation that happens often. So yes, it's a possibility, but I can't be sure anything, not until we decide to do this—*if* we decide to do it."

Ulric wasn't sure how to feel about this. He wanted Sky to bond with him, of course, and he didn't care why it happened. It would be great if Sky fell in love with him and decided he wanted to spend the rest of his life with him, but Ulric would take pretty much anything.

He knew it was too soon for either of them to care about the other the way mates did. They weren't in love, but Ulric was a shifter, and he'd hoped this would happen for decades. He knew they would fall in love eventually. He wasn't afraid of bonding with Sky for the wrong reasons, not when he was sure they'd become the right ones given time.

But Sky was human, or at least, he'd been human until recently. Even if he *had* thought about being a shifter's mate, he might not have thought like a shifter. Humans didn't expect to bond right away. They wanted to date, to get to know each other, and they weren't wrong. Being mates wasn't a miracle fix for everything. Mates still fought, they still had problems. But with work, being mates and sharing a bond could be the best thing in the world.

"I don't know," Sky said. "I want to say yes both because I feel I need help with the control thing and because, well, we're mates."

"You don't have to say yes because of anything. I already told you I don't expect anything from you, even though I'd like for you to give us a chance. But I understand you have to be focused on other things right now, and that's okay."

Sky gently slapped Ulric's arm. "Can I finish?"

"Of course." Ulric had to force himself not to smile. He found Sky adorable, but especially so now that he'd started relaxing with him. He was truer to himself, and that was what Ulric wanted. Sky should feel comfortable with him, much more than with anyone else.

Sky cleared his throat. "What I was trying to say is that I want to explore the bond between us. I don't know if I'm ready to bond yet in a relationship sense, because we haven't known each other that long, and I'm also not sure if I want to bond only to help with my control problem. Part of me wants to say yes because this is hard, but I'd feel like I would take advantage of you if I did because it would only partly because I want to be with you."

"Can I talk now?"

Sky narrowed his eyes. "Yes."

"There isn't a right reason for you to decide to bond with me."

"That's bullshit. It's obvious that if you want to bond with me, it's because you want a future with me, and I'm not talking about being friends."

"I don't want to only be friends, that's true. But I also don't think that bonding to help you would be a bad thing. I wouldn't have suggested it otherwise. I believe we'll fall in love, so how we begin this relationship doesn't matter. I want to do what I can to help you, and this is it, or at least, I think so."

Sky bit his lower lip. "I don't know if I share that opinion."

"You don't have to. Look, think about it. Even if we do decide to bond, it's not going to work miracles. You'll still have to work hard, but that's why we're here."

Ulric rose from his chair and left Sky in front of the fire to think. He might as well start dinner. He and Sky were going to have to share a tent tonight, and that would have been awkward even without Sky's problem. They'd have to find a way around it, because Ulric wasn't planning on waking up with the tent on fire.

"I know this isn't much, but we'll have to make do with this for now," he said as he brought the sausages and the container of potato salad to the fire. He'd had to raid the fridge at home, since they'd decided to leave without planning. Hopefully, Dasha would be back with more food soon. "But this is good. Graham is a great cook, and he always keeps a lot of leftovers in the fridge for us to eat."

Sky smiled.

Ulric wasn't sure, but he thought his mate looked more relaxed.

"That's perfectly fine."

They roasted the sausages over the fire and ate pretty much in silence. They both had a lot of things to think about, but especially Sky. Ulric had already made his decision. If Sky thought it would help, if it was what he wanted, Ulric wanted to bond with him. He wasn't the only one who had to make that decision, though, and he didn't want to push Sky into anything he might regret. Sky could be a romantic, someone who wanted to bond as a sign of love, like marriage. Some shifters were like that, and most humans were, too.

If he was honest with himself, Ulric had often thought he'd bond for love. He wanted to, but it wasn't that big of a deal for him.

They cleaned up together, still silent, and Ulric was starting to get nervous. He wasn't sure Sky had realized they were going to have to sleep together, but if he hadn't, that would change soon.

When Ulric came back from doing his business in the forest, Sky was standing in front of the tent, his hands on his hips, staring at it. He didn't look pleased, and Ulric thought he'd probably realized what was about to happen.

"Are you trying to set it on fire with your gaze?" he asked.

Sky jerked toward him. "I hadn't thought about it. We can't share the tent, though."

"Why not?"

"Because things generally don't end well when I'm close to you."

"You mean you might set it on fire?"

"Exactly. I've never caught fire while I was sleeping, but it's not a risk I want to take."

Ulric crouched next to the tent and dragged the two sleeping bags outside. "How about this? We can sleep outside, but I want us to sleep close. You need to get used to my presence."

Sky looked hesitant, but he nodded. Ulric took care of setting everything up while Sky took his time in the forest, and when he came back, Ulric was on his back in his sleeping bag. He patted the other one, which was so close they might as well have been sharing one. Sky looked from the sleeping bag to Ulric, then back, huffed, and finally took his shoes off.

It took him a few minutes to find a comfortable spot, and once he did, both he and Ulric were facing the sky.

"This is weird," Sky murmured.

"I don't feel weird."

"I spent the past year alone in a cell. Everything is weird to me right now."

Ulric propped himself up on an elbow and looked down at Sky. His brown hair had fanned around him, and it looked soft. Ulric wanted to touch it, and since Sky needed to get used to him, he did.

Sky tensed, but he didn't move away. Ulric swallowed. He knew he was about to risk a lot, but this was what Sky needed to get better — and what they both wanted. "I'm going to kiss you."

Sky's eyes widened. "I don't think that's a wise idea. You do remember what happened the last time you did it, right?"

"I do. But unless you don't want me to kiss you, I'm going to do it."

Sky sucked in a breath, but he didn't push Ulric away when

Ulric leaned closer. Their lips brushed together, and Ulric stopped to give Sky a few seconds. When nothing happened, Ulric kissed Sky again, deeper this time. "Relax. Try to keep your emotions under control."

Sky snorted. "That's easier said than done."

"I know, but I have faith in you. You can do this."

And he did. There were a few close calls, but Ulric was pressed against Sky, and he could feel him becoming warmer as the fire built inside him. He was able to help Sky to keep the fire under control, and he counted that as a win.

He also counted the way Sky fell asleep wrapped around him as a win.

CHAPTER SIX

Sky hated the forest. He hated camping. He wanted to go home, even though he had no idea where home was to him.

It had been two weeks. Two long, excruciating weeks, and he still wasn't anywhere close to having enough control over his ability to not be a danger to anyone.

He didn't know what to do. He'd been working his ass off for the past couple of weeks, but he might as well not have. That was how many results he'd had.

"Things aren't as dire as you make them," Ulric said.

Sky glared at him. He wanted to kick Ulric's chair to the ground, but of course, he didn't do it. It was his frustration talking, nothing more. "Of course you'd say that. I haven't set you on fire yet." But he had set a tree on fire, as well as a few bushes, and one time, the tent. Luckily for them, they'd managed to control the fire before it took down their only home in the woods, but Sky was still uncomfortable with his ability, and he didn't know what he had to do to get it under full control.

"Look, you finally managed to have enough control to only set what you want on fire. I don't understand why you're so angry."

Sky was miffed because he might have control over his ability, but that control stopped when Ulric touched him. Ulric always made him lose control, and that was a bad thing because Sky *really* wanted to fuck him.

He had no idea what he had to do to make that happen. Sleeping next to Ulric every night was maddening, especially when they did nothing more than kissing. Sky supposed he should be happy they did at least that, considering they'd almost lost one of the sleeping bags a few days ago while making out. But spending so much time with Ulric with no way to escape his presence was driving Sky crazy.

It wasn't only physical, although he couldn't deny that was part of it. But Sky knew he was falling in love with Ulric, and he didn't want it to stop. Ulric cared for him. He could so easily have stayed back home, but instead, he put himself in danger every day to help Sky get his ability and his life under control. And it wasn't just that. Ulric always cooked Sky breakfast because Sky liked to stay in bed — or in this case, in his sleeping bag — for as long as he could. Every morning, Ulric put their sleeping bags back in the tent, and every night, he took them out and made sure there were no pebbles or whatever else under them that might make Sky uncomfortable. They were small gestures, but Sky couldn't ignore them or ignore what they meant.

"I don't want to set you on fire," Sky whined.

"You haven't yet."

"You make that sound like a victory."

Ulric shrugged. He looked like he belonged in the forest. He'd just come back from a run in his wolf form, and Sky wished he could have gone with him. He hadn't gone anywhere near the forest except to use the bathroom, though. He didn't want to risk setting the entire thing on fire and killing both of them. Not that he'd die in a fire, but he wasn't sure he'd be able to face life if something happened to Ulric because of him.

"It *is* a victory," Ulric said. "We've been making out and touching every day. You've had plenty of opportunities to set me on fire, but I've only had a few burns."

And those were a few too many in Sky's opinion. He'd tried pushing Ulric away after the first time he had burned him, but Ulric wasn't having any of that. He didn't seem to want distance between them, no matter how many times he got burned. He was resilient, and he had so much faith in Sky and what he could do that Sky felt awed. He wasn't sure *he* had that much faith in himself, and he didn't understand how Ulric could.

"The only thing you can do is to continue training and forcing yourself to do better," Ulric continued.

Sky knew he could eventually be as good as Cora, but he had no idea how long it was going to take him, and he wasn't about to spend the winter in the woods. What other option did he have, though?

He could go back to the warehouse where the assassins lived. No one would say no to having him there, and they wouldn't kick him out. He could move back into the fireproof rooms and spend most of his time there training. That would feel like he was giving up, though, and he wasn't going to do that.

Sky swallowed and looked at his hands. He could feel the fire burning under his skin, ready to jump out if Sky needed it. But Sky *didn't* need it, and that was the problem. He needed the fire to stay under his skin unless he consciously wanted it to come out. He couldn't imagine a situation in which he'd want that to happen, but there was no getting rid of it.

Ulric sighed. "Sky, you've been working hard. You've been doing everything you can to learn control, and it's working. It's obvious I'm your weak link, but we can continue working on that, and you'll see, you'll get great at this eventually."

Sky huffed. "Eventually isn't soon enough. I want to be good at it *now*." Because he wanted to fuck Ulric. He wasn't about to say that to Ulric's face, even though he knew Ulric shared that emotion.

"Have you thought about what we talked about when we got here?"

Ulric sounded oddly hesitant, which was enough to tell Sky what he was talking about.

Of course he'd thought about bonding with Ulric. Some days, it felt like he couldn't think about anything else. He still felt like saying yes would be taking advantage of Ulric, but things were different now, weren't they? Sky had liked Ulric those first few days, but it was more than that now.

He was happy. Even though he hated sleeping rough and using the forest as a bathroom, there was no denying that, just like there was no denying that Ulric was a big part of that happiness. They didn't spend all of their time training, and when they weren't, they talked.

They talked about everything, from how Sky imagine his future to be to what their favorite bands were, or even their favorite colors. Sky knew Ulric. He knew Ulric was a good man, a man it would be easy to spend the rest of his life with, especially when he was already falling in love with him.

So would bonding with him still be taking advantage of him?

Sky didn't think so. His reason for bonding with Ulric had shifted over the past couple of weeks. It was true the bond might help with his control, but that wasn't the main reason Sky wanted it anymore.

This was why he'd wanted to wait, and he knew he'd done the right thing. Neither he nor Ulric had brought this up again until now, but now Ulric had, and he was waiting for an answer.

Sky didn't doubt that he could stay vague and Ulric wouldn't push. Ulric was like that. He needed Sky to be happy, even if it made him unhappy. He'd given up a lot to stay in the woods with Sky for weeks. He was ready to give up even more if that was what Sky needed or wanted. When they'd talked about his job, Ulric had made it clear that he was ready to quit if that was what Sky wanted, if he wanted to move away from the warehouse.

Sky knew he didn't have to become an assassin to stay there. Ulric had been clear about that, and Sky was relieved, because he didn't think he'd ever be able to hurt someone on purpose. He knew he had options, but for some reason, when he thought of the future, he could only imagine himself living with Ulric and the assassins. They were Ulric's family, and Sky knew they'd welcome him with open arms, just like they had when he'd first arrived there.

Ulric's cell phone vibrated. He looked down at it, smiling. "Dasha is here. I asked him to bring ice cream with the groceries, so get comfortable, because we're eating it as soon as I'm back."

Dasha had taken to shimmering between the trees. Sky wasn't sure why, but Ulric had looked worried a few times after talking to his friend, and Sky wanted them to have the opportunity to be alone and talk if that was what they needed. He never pushed to go with Ulric, and Ulric never asked.

Sky watched him walk away, his mind still wondering if this was it. He wanted to bond, and so did Ulric. They needed to talk about it, but since they both wanted the same thing, Sky was pretty sure it was going to happen today.

Dasha still looked tired and sad. Ulric didn't understand it, and no matter how many times he asked, Dasha never gave him a straight answer. Ulric knew something was wrong, and he wanted to find out what it was and help Dasha if he needed him, but most of his focus was on Sky, and that couldn't change, not for now. Ulric but didn't know what to do, and he knew pushing wouldn't make Dasha change his mind about telling him what was going on.

"Everything okay at home?" Uric asked.

Dasha held out the two plastic bags he was holding.

"Yeah."

"You two?"

"Of course."

Ulric wasn't going to call him out on it. He'd already told Dasha he could talk to him if he needed to plenty of times. Dasha knew that. When he was ready, he'd come to Ulric or any of their other friends. "Thank you for doing this."

Dasha blinked. "Doing what? Keeping you fed? You don't need to thank me for that."

"I don't see why not. Sky and I wouldn't be here if it weren't for you."

"Maybe not, but I wanted to help. You're doing the right thing helping him."

"I know. Still, I can't wait to go home. I'm starting to miss my bathroom." Ulric didn't have a problem cleaning his fur with his tongue or using wipes to keep his human body stink-less, but there was something to say about a nice shower.

"How is Sky doing?"

"Surprisingly well, to be honest. He's angry that he still doesn't have enough control where I'm concerned, but I'm not surprised."

"You're mates. Of course you make him emotional."

"Exactly." Ulric peeked into the bags. "Did you bring everything I asked for?"

"Yes. Ice cream, chocolate, and a few more pillows."

"Thank you. Seriously, as soon as I'm back, ask me whatever you want or need, and it's yours."

"I only want you to take care of your mate."

There was something there, but Ulric didn't know what it was. Why did Dasha sound sad at the mention of mates and taking care of them? Ulric didn't have answers, and he didn't have the time to ask for them. "Text me if you need anything," he said even though Dasha already knew it.

Dasha patted Ulric's shoulder. "I will. Now bring your

mate his ice cream."

Ulric didn't like leaving Dasha behind, but when he turned to look back at him, Dasha had left. Ulric had no idea where he'd gone, if it was home or somewhere else, and he was worried. He moved one of the bags so he was holding both of them in one hand and took his phone out, quickly texting Lawrence to ask him to keep an eye on Dasha. He didn't wait for Lawrence to answer and put his phone back in his pocket before heading to the tent where Sky was waiting for him.

But Sky wasn't. When Ulric got there, Sky was facing the other way, focused on the fire pit. As Ulric watched, Sky set the wood in the pit on fire, then snuffed it out again. He repeated that a few times before Ulric decided to interrupt him.

"That's great," Ulric said.

Sky jumped, and both his hands caught fire. Ulric stayed as still as he could until he was sure Sky realized what had happened. Sky scowled, and the fire disappeared. "What the fuck were you thinking?"

Ulric was surprised at how angry Sky was. "I didn't mean to scare you."

"Maybe not, but you did. I could have hurt you."

"I'm sorry. I thought you knew I was about to come back. I just picked up the groceries."

Sky raked a hand through his hair. "I know. But you didn't come back right away, and I wasn't sure how long you'd be, so I decided to train."

Ulric put the bags down and took out the ice cream and two spoons he'd asked Dasha to put in there. "I saw, and it was great. You have so much more control on your fire than you had in the beginning."

"Except when you're around."

"Yes, but I'm sure you'll be able to get over that. Would you have imagined being able to do what you just did a few weeks ago?"

Sky's shoulders slumped. "I wouldn't have, no."

Ulric handed him one of the spoons, and they settled into their chairs. "So you're admitting you're better?" Sky hadn't yet. No matter how many times Ulric pointed out how good he was becoming at controlling his ability, Sky refused to see it. He was so focused on being able to control himself when he was kissing Ulric that he ignored everything else.

Sky snatched the ice cream from Ulric's hands. "Okay, I admit it. I did get better. Not where it counts, but I guess it's something."

"Not where it counts? What are you talking about? I thought you wanted to learn control so you could get your life back."

"Of course I do. I'm tired of the woods. I want a shower, hell, a *bath*. I want to be able to open the fridge and eat what I want when I want."

Ulric's stomach churned. "We can go home if you want. You have more than enough control right now that you can live with us without a problem."

Sky's eyes narrowed. "Maybe, but I don't have enough control to be around you, and that's the most important thing."

"Is it?"

Sky stuffed a spoonful of ice cream into his mouth.

Ulric snatched the container from him.

"It became the most important thing as soon as I realized how I felt about you," Sky finally said.

Ulric's brain felt like it was frozen, but he wasn't sure if it was because of the ice cream or because of Sky's words. "How you feel?"

"You have to realize I like you."

He did. It would have been impossible to ignore, considering how close they'd become over the past couple weeks. It wasn't just the kissing, although Ulric couldn't deny he loved that. But they'd talked a lot, and he was starting to understand Sky. He was beginning to fall in love with his mate, and he was over the moon about that. Now if only Sky's ability would cooperate, they could maybe start their new life together, whatever that entailed.

Ulric cleared his throat. "I like you, too."

Sky chuckled. "I sure hope so, considering we're mates and that I've been thinking about what you talked about."

Ulric didn't want to hope, just in case he didn't understand what Sky was talking about. "Yes?"

"You just mentioned it, although not in that many words. But I've been doing a lot of thinking, just as I'm sure you have."

Ulric *had* to ask. "About bonding?"

Sky licked his spoon. "You *really* think it's going to help me?"

Ulric leaned back in his chair. He wasn't sure how to answer that. Sky already knew he wasn't a hundred percent convinced that would be the case, but they both hoped it would. It was the last piece of the puzzle, the only thing they needed to be able to go back to their life.

Ulric thought he was going to miss this time, though. He knew Sky wasn't crazy about camping, but he didn't mind it, lack of shower notwithstanding. His wolf had been more than happy, and so had Ulric. When was he ever going to have this much time alone with Sky again? It wouldn't be possible, especially not in the house. But it wasn't fair of him to keep Sky to himself, and he knew it. Sky had been alone for too long when he'd been in the lab. He needed to make friends and start living again. Ulric felt lucky Sky wanted him in his life, and he had to make sure not to clip his wings.

"I hope so. It's obvious that the only problem you still have left is me. I'm hoping to be able to help you through our bond by showing you how it feels when I exert control over my ability, and that being able to feel me will help you." It could also make things harder, but at that point, Ulric doubted things could go worse.

"But we can't be sure until we do it."

"No, we can't. But I want you to know that the reason I have to bond with you doesn't have anything to do with your ability, not anymore. It would be great if it helped you, but honestly, I just want you in my life. I want us to be together, to become one." Just like Ulric had dreamed of when he was a teenager.

Sky nodded. "All right."

Ulric blinked. "All right?"

"I want us to bond."

Sky wasn't sure why he was so nervous. He already knew what Ulric's answer would be, or at least, he thought he did. Ulric had been clear when they'd talked about bonding earlier—he wanted them to bond, and he didn't care about the reason behind Sky's decision to do it. Still, he looked surprised, and that was enough for Sky to feel uncomfortable.

Maybe Ulric had changed his mind. Maybe he'd decided it would be better to wait. Maybe he wanted Sky to bond with him for love and not because it would be easier for him to control his ability. Maybe—

"All right."

Sky blinked. "Okay?" he repeated.

Ulric smiled. "I thought that was the answer you wanted from me."

"Of course it's the answer I want, but I don't want you to feel like you have to say yes."

"We've already been over this, Sky. I want us to bond. I *am* curious about why you've decided now was the right moment to do it, but I'm not going to say no."

Sky looked down. He'd been training when Ulric had come back with the groceries, and it had been going well, at least until Ulric had arrived. Sky couldn't say that Ulric's presence had made a mess, but it might have if he hadn't been able to control himself. He'd almost burned Ulric to a crisp because he'd been surprised, and he didn't like that. If bonding with Ulric meant he could be aware of where his mate was and prepared in case something like that happened again, then Sky was all for it.

Of course, he also hoped that being bonded meant they could have sex. He felt like an idiot for feeling like that, but there was no denying that spending so much time alone with Ulric was frustrating. Sky hadn't even been able to sneak away to jack off because Ulric would have noticed. Sky wasn't sure Ulric would have said anything about it, but he hadn't wanted to risk it. That meant he hadn't come in two weeks, even though he slept every night tangled with the hottest man he'd ever met, and said man was his mate.

"I like you," Sky said. He needed Ulric to be aware of that.

"You're ready told me that, too. I know you like me, and I like you."

Sky shook his head. "You don't understand. When I say like you, I mean that I'm falling in love with you." Sky felt incredibly vulnerable admitting that, but he couldn't back down. He needed Ulric to know how he felt, to know he wasn't choosing to bond with him to take advantage of the bond and nothing else. That was part of it, of course, and they both knew it, but it wasn't the most important part, not anymore.

"I'm falling in love with you, too, Sky."

Ulric's voice was quiet, barely more than a whisper, but it felt like he'd shouted the words. Sky's heart stuttered, and he forced himself to look up, because there was nothing for him to be ashamed off, and he hadn't been rejected. Ulric wanted him, just like he wanted Ulric. Sky's ability had moved to the back burner for now, and that was okay. Sky was relieved he could forget about it for a while. That hadn't happened since he had been in his cell in the lab and had killed the guard.

Sky cleared his throat. "Okay then. I guess we should do this."

Ulric laughed and tilted his chin at the bags he'd put down next to the chairs. "How about we have dinner first? I asked Dasha to bring chocolate and more pillows. I know you've been uncomfortable sleeping on the ground."

Sky's heart melted. Ulric always thought about him, no matter what happens. Sky couldn't remember any other of his boyfriends acting this way, and at this point, he didn't care if it was because Ulric was just that kind of man or because of the bond. It didn't matter. The bond was in them and thinking about what it could influence and what it couldn't wouldn't change a thing. "Okay. What do you need me to do?"

"I'd tell you to relax, but I already know what you're going to tell me about that."

Damn right he knew. He'd tried doing everything in the beginning, as if Sky was too fragile to even wash the dishes in the small stream that ran close to their camp. Sky had quickly pointed out that he was just as capable as Ulric of cooking and doing chores, and Ulric had given up, thankfully. Sky hated feeling helpless, and Ulric's behavior hadn't been helping.

They worked together, comfortable and familiar with each other. They'd been doing this for two weeks, but it felt like much longer, and Sky couldn't help but wonder how they'd move around each other in two years, or two decades.

Ulric was a shifter. Sky didn't know if what had been done to him in the lab had extended his life, but even if it hadn't, bonding with Ulric would. He wasn't sure how he felt about watching his family growing old and die while he still looked pretty much the same, but that wasn't going to be enough to stop him. He'd have to learn to deal with it, just like every human bonded to shifters did.

But Sky couldn't deny he was nervous. He knew how bonding worked, of course. Everyone knew it now that shifters didn't hide anymore. He wasn't afraid of the bite, even though he wasn't looking forward to the drinking blood part. He could also do without the pain, but he'd learned pain during his time in the lab, and this would be a happy one. It wouldn't be a problem.

But for some reason, Sky felt awkward. He and Ulric had gotten used to living together, but this was different. Even though they'd kissed every day, they hadn't done anything else, and they hadn't behaved like a couple. It was entirely Sky's fault, of course, and now Sky regretted it.

He'd known Ulric wanted more. He'd wanted more, too. But he'd been afraid to hurt Ulric, and keeping some distance between them had made him feel better. They'd kissed, but Sky always had to be hypervigilant when they did, and he didn't think he could have spent the entire day like that. He didn't know how things were going to work once they were bonded, but he supposed he was about to find out.

Dinner was silent, and this time, when Ulric told Sky to go wash up and leave the dishes to him, Sky didn't protest. He needed some time alone to gather his thoughts and think.

He wasn't going to change his mind. He'd thought about it long enough, and he was convinced of his choice. But bonding was still like getting married, and it was a huge decision anyone would be nervous about. Sky's stomach churned, both because he wasn't sure what to expect, how he and Ulric were going to do this, and because of the impact bonding would have on his life.

Sky's life had changed so much over the past year that sometimes he had trouble keeping up with everything. He'd been taken from his home, from his family, and locked up.

He'd been experimented on, and he wasn't human anymore. He had an ability he couldn't fully control, and he'd met his mate. He needed life to slow down, and he hoped that would happen once he and Ulric were bonded.

Sky quickly stripped when he got to the stream. He hadn't allowed himself to do that in the beginning because he'd been afraid that someone would see him, but in two weeks, no one had come. This was an isolated place, and he was grateful for that. It was time to relax when he didn't expect someone to surprise him every second of the day.

The stream wasn't large, but it was enough for Sky to stretch on his back and be almost entirely submerged. The water was cold, but Sky felt like he needed that right now. Dasha had brought some bio soap and shampoo a few days after Sky and Ulric had arrived, so Sky used them to get clean. He wasn't sure he'd ever be able to get the scent of the forest out of his hair, but he didn't mind it. He soaped his hands and ran them over his body, doing more than one pass under his armpits and on his groin, then hesitating when he got to his ass.

He had no idea what Ulric had in mind. Were they only going to bond, or were they also going to have sex? Sky knew what he wanted, but they hadn't talked about it. Just in case, he wanted to be prepared, so he quickly stretched himself, wincing at the sensation. It hurt a bit, probably because he hadn't had sex in way too long, but he didn't care. He felt like he was about to explode, and his cock was half hard once he was clean and dressed again.

It was getting dark, so he rushed back to camp. He knew Ulric was probably done cleaning up after dinner, so he wasn't surprised to find his mate stretched out on the sleeping bags by the fire. Ulric was still clothed, and Sky stopped by his feet, looking down at him.

"All clean?" Ulric asked.

Sky nodded and swallowed. *What now?*

Ulric wasn't surprised to see Sky hesitant. He knew it had nothing to do with the decision Sky had made but probably with what they were about to do. Bonding was a massive change in one's life, no matter whether they were human or shifters. Sky also had the added stress of his ability not being under control, and that wasn't helping.

It made Ulric nervous, too. He wasn't looking forward to being naked under the stars, but he was pretty sure it was the safest option. Neither he nor Sky knew how Sky would react to bonding, and Ulric didn't wish to risk the tent. They could always go home and get another one, but he'd rather avoid that. North would laugh until Christmas if he found out.

"Why don't you sit down next to me?" Ulric said as he sat up.

Sky stared at him for another few seconds, then reached for the bottom of his t-shirt. He quickly stripped, and Ulric wasn't sure whether or not he was allowed to watch. He wanted to, just like he'd wanted to for the past two weeks, but Sky had only ever stripped at the stream, and Ulric had given him the privacy he wanted. But now Sky was getting naked in front of him, and they were about to bond. Bonding didn't always go along with sex, but it usually did.

They should probably have talked about this when they'd talked about bonding.

Watching Sky seemingly so sure of himself was arousing, though. Ulric suspected that the reason Sky was stripping right now was that he was afraid of backing out of it if he didn't. Sky was an odd and utterly lovable mix of self-consciousness and strength, and he alternated between them. Right now, it looked like he wanted to get this out of the way, and he'd gone straight to the point.

Sky flopped onto the sleeping bag next to Ulric's. He made

sure to keep his groin covered, but Ulric could see the tip of his cock peeking from above his hands. "What now?"

Ulric forced himself to look at Sky's face, even though he wanted nothing more than to explore his mate's body. Sky was gorgeous, made for Ulric's hands, and it had been hell not touching him for the past two weeks, especially when they'd been making out so much. "I think we should bond first. That is, if you want to do anything else, of course. I mean, you don't *have* to do anything else." *Dammit.* Ulric had thought about this. He'd even put together a little speech to tell Sky they didn't have to do anything more than bonding.

For some reason, Ulric's blathering seemed to amuse Sky. "Trust me. I want to do more than bonding."

"Oh, good. I mean, I want to do more than bonding too, but I would have been okay with you wanting only that."

Sky relaxed.

Ulric didn't enjoy feeling like a fool, but if that was the result, he didn't mind that much.

"You want to bond first?"

"Yes." There was a reason for that, but it took Ulric a few seconds to remember it, because he couldn't stop thinking about having sex with Sky. He cleared his throat. "Sex is probably going to be the hardest part for you. You even lose control when we're only kissing, so I want to be sure we have everything on your side to help you with control when we do it — *if* we do it. Because like I said, we don't have to."

Sky rolled his eyes. "Stop worrying about that. I want to fuck you. Trust me."

"Okay, perfect."

Sky arched a brow. "I suspect things would be easier if you stripped down, too. You don't have to get naked if you'd rather not, but at least your t-shirt so we can bond?"

He was right. Ulric couldn't remember the last time he'd felt so flustered, but he was sure it had been with Sky. No one else had this effect on him, and he didn't want them to.

He took his t-shirt off, then hesitated and decided *fuck it*. He'd left his boots next to the sleeping bag, so he only had to take care of his jeans, underwear, and socks. He'd washed in the stream earlier after he'd come back from his run in his wolf form, so he was clean enough.

Then they were both naked. Ulric felt a bit like it was his first time, and in a way, it was. Sex had never felt like this. It wasn't supposed to. Sex was good, of course, but with his mate, it would be phenomenal.

"Where are you going to bite me?" Sky asked.

Ulric leaned toward him and gently touched the spot where his neck met his shoulder. "Here, if you're okay with it."

"I am. Am I supposed to bite you?"

"You can, of course, but for people without fangs, it's usually easier if I cut my throat and you just suck the blood."

Sky wrinkled his nose. "That sounds terrible."

Ulric couldn't deny it did, but it was the only way for them to bond. He moved even closer to Sky, and to his surprise, Sky stretched out on his back. He opened his arms in welcome, and Ulric didn't hesitate.

He pressed their bodies together, lying half on top of Sky, half on the sleeping bag. He hooked a leg between Sky's and nosed the crook of Sky's neck.

"Is it going to hurt?" Sky asked.

"A bit." Ulric couldn't promise it wouldn't hurt, so he was quick about it, cutting his own neck with a shifted nail, then pressing his mouth against Sky's skin and biting down. Sky's blood filled Ulric's mouth, and Ulric drank it down. He could feel Sky doing the same on his neck, and he shuddered in pleasure. Blood was blood, and it didn't taste good, but it was life and bond and love.

Ulric was hard against Sky, and he pressed even closer as

the bond between them sparked into life. It had already been there, but now, it was a strong, so strong that nothing would break it.

He could feel what Sky wanted. Sky was hesitant, worried, but he wanted Ulric as much as Ulric wanted him. He'd wrapped himself around Ulric as they drank each other's blood, and Ulric thanked God, or in this case, Dasha, who had thought about putting lube into one of the grocery bags he'd brought the first week.

Ulric had stuck the bottle under his sleeping bag, and he blindly looked for it with his hand as he sealed the bite on Sky's throat shut and turned his head to kiss his mate. His lips met Sky's, and they both tasted of blood, warm and coppery, yet so good. Ulric's fingers closed on the bottle, and he rolled, pulling Sky on top of him. Sky yelped and held down, glaring down at Ulric as he straddled Ulric's hips, Ulric's cock pressing between Sky's ass cheeks.

"What are you doing?"

Ulric grinned. He held out the bottle where Sky could see it. "I thought it was obvious."

Sky's gaze flickered to the lube, then back to Ulric's face. "You thought you were going to score?"

"I hoped I would. I've wanted you since that first day."

"I was all dirty and probably looked like a madman."

Ulric drew Sky closer. "You were beautiful, and you still are."

Sky snatched the lube from Ulric's hand. He opened the bottle and squirted a good amount on his fingers. He reached behind himself, and Ulric held his breath. "We can do it the other way around, if you want," Ulric suggested. He didn't want Sky to feel like he had to do this. That was one more thing they should have discussed before taking this step.

Sky glared again. "I want your cock in my ass. I've been dreaming about this moment for the past two weeks, and damn if I'm going to do this the other way around. That can wait for next time."

Ulric couldn't wait, and he hoped the next time would be tonight, or maybe tomorrow morning. He reached for Sky, moving one of his hands around Sky's back, but Sky batted his hands away. "I'm already stretched. I just need to stick lube in there so it doesn't hurt."

Ulric arched a brow. "You thought you were going to score?" he asked, throwing Sky's words back at him.

"Shut up."

And Ulric did, because Sky chose that moment to wrap his fingers around Ulric's cock and lower himself onto it.

Sky was warm and tight and *home*. The fact that Ulric could feel Sky's emotions looping with his made everything overwhelming yet so good. It was perfect, and Ulric wouldn't have changed anything as Sky moved on top of him.

Well, maybe he would have done without the sparks of fire that Sky couldn't seem to be able to snuff out from his skin, but he was too far gone to care much.

That proved to be a mistake.

Ulric had already been close to orgasm after he and Sky had bonded, so he didn't take long for him to come. He made sure Sky was right there with him, pulling on Sky's cock and pressing up into him as Sky pushed down. Ulric felt the moment Sky came. Sky tightened around him, milking his cock, and he thrust harder and deeper, filling Sky with his cum.

That was when Sky caught fire.

His entire body burned, setting fire to the sleeping bags, the clothes they'd left close by, and even the tent, with everything inside it. Sky panicked and started getting up, but Ulric stopped him, pressing him down again.

"What are you doing?" Sky asked, panic tingeing his words.

"I'm not burning." Ulric didn't know how it was possible,

but Sky's fire wasn't hurting him.

Sky blinked and looked down. He was still sitting on top of Ulric, with Ulric's cock inside him, and Ulric was touching him. Ulric should have been burned to hell and back by now, but he wasn't. He raised his hands so Sky could see them, could see that they *weren't* burned.

The fire disappeared. Sky's eyes were wide as he took in the fact that Ulric was okay. "I was terrified."

Ulric had been, too. "I'm okay."

"How is that possible?"

"I don't know. The bond, probably." That was the only thing Ulric could think of, the only thing that changed since Sky had last burned him.

"You're immune to my fire now?"

"I think so." Ulric rolled his head. "But the tent wasn't, and neither were our clothes." Luckily for them, Ulric had left his phone turned off and in a plastic bag in a tree close by. He'd learned when Sky had almost burned it once. Still, Ulric wasn't looking forward to calling Dasha and asking him to bring clothes because Sky had burned everything they'd brought with them.

CHAPTER SEVEN

Sky was starting to regret this. What on earth had possessed him to ask to meet with Griffith's father? He'd thought it would be a good idea to face the man responsible for what he was now, but at the moment, watching him through the window, Sky wondered if he'd been wrong.

He didn't want to talk to Gavin White. He wanted to forget everything that had happened when he'd been in the lab. But he wanted to put his past where it belonged — behind him. Bonding with Ulric had helped, but Sky still needed answers. He wasn't sure he'd get them, but at least he'd be able to say he'd tried.

"You don't need to do this," Ulric said.

"I know."

"But I'm here if you need me."

Sky was grateful Ulric hadn't attempted to dissuade him. He'd done enough of that on his own. "Thank you."

Ulric had suggested he could go in with Sky, but Sky didn't want anyone in there with him. It would be dangerous for anyone but Ulric, and in Ulric's case, Sky had been tempted to say yes. But he needed to do this on his own. He was finally standing on his own two feet again, and that needed to continue.

He'd been stunned at how easy control came to him after he'd come back from his two-week camping trip with Ulric. The basics had already been there, thanks to Cora and Tony, and once Sky had realized he couldn't hurt Ulric anymore, it had been easier to control the ability. Sky realized it was

117

weird, but the block that had been there, the fear and panic that always made him freak out when he thought about Ulric being hurt, were gone. He didn't have to be afraid he'd hurt Ulric anymore, and that made him more relaxed, and in turn, it was easier for him to control himself.

If he'd known that was what he needed to make this work, he'd have bonded with Ulric that first night.

"Ready when you are," Win said.

Sky doubted he'd ever be ready to face the monster who had changed his life so much, but he nodded anyway. He swallowed then reached for the door that would lead him into the interrogation room.

He did his best to stay calm as he walked in and closed the door behind him. Griffith's father looked at him, a frown on his face. Sky didn't think he recognized him. Why should he? He hadn't worked on Sky. He hadn't been there when Sky had killed the guard. He hadn't been the one who'd taken Sky, but that didn't make him any less responsible.

Sky sat at the table facing a frowning Gavin White.

"Who are you?" Gavin asked.

Sky leaned his fingers together on top of the table. "One would think you'd remember me, considering you had me kidnapped and had scientists manipulate my DNA."

Gavin paled, but he kept his back straight. "I don't remember everyone who passed through my lab."

"I don't think that's a good thing to say, Gavin, especially not to me." Sky extended a hand and released the fire.

This time, Gavin jerked back as far as he could. He was handcuffed to the table, though, so he wasn't going anywhere. Sky stayed where he was and made the fire flicker. It would be so easy to burn Gavin, to let go of the control Sky had and let the fire do what it did best. That wasn't Sky, though.

He turned the fire off. "I want to know who you work

with."

"I already told the others. I worked for the government."

"We want names." Gavin had already given those to Win, but Win wanted to see if confronting one of the people he'd hurt would push Gavin into saying more than he had. Besides, Sky felt like this was the moment in which he would leave his painful past behind and finally focus on the future, and he needed that.

Sky didn't have to tell Gavin what he risked if he didn't give him the answers he wanted. The man didn't know that Sky didn't have it in him to burn him, and Sky wanted to keep that as it was. He took a piece of paper and a crayon out of his pocket and put them onto the table before pushing them toward Gavin. "Start writing."

Gavin hesitated, but they both knew there was no way out of this for him. He would give names. Otherwise, Sky would burn him.

Or so Gavin thought.

"Where did you get us?" Sky asked as Gavin finally started writing.

Gavin looked up. "What do you mean?"

"It's obvious we want the names of your superiors, considering your lab shouldn't have existed. But I'm also curious to know where you got the humans and shifters you experimented on. I doubt you were the one kidnapping us off the streets." And none of the scientists who'd worked in the lab would have been able to do that, either. Maybe the guards, but Sky wasn't convinced.

"The Beasts, of course."

"Only them?" Sky tapped his fingertips onto the table, creating a spark.

Gavin's gaze went to them, and he paled even more. "There was someone else."

Of course there was. Even though Gavin's operation hadn't

been big, it *had* been big enough for him to need help. He couldn't count on the government, since the operation was a secret, so he'd had to find help elsewhere. "I want names." Sky tilted his chin toward the piece of paper, and Gavin got back to work.

"He's building an army, or at least, that's what he wants to do," Gavin said.

"Who is?"

"His name is Elroy Miller. He's a shifter, a wolf shifter. I don't know all the details, but his brother was the alpha of a pack in California. I don't know if his brother died or was arrested, but I do know that the pack doesn't exist anymore, because the council dismantled it. Elroy wants to get revenge on the council."

"And where do you fall in this story?"

"He wants an army. He supplied shifters and humans we could use to experiment on and turn into fighters, and I agreed to give him one of each that made it through."

"And your boss was okay with that?"

"He didn't know. He wants an army, too, and he couldn't care less about the people who would get hurt. Neither of them does."

Sky snorted. "Because you do? Shut up and write. I want all the names you can give me, your boss', and Elroy's."

Sky leaned back in his chair. He'd been told about the group of people who'd tried killing the assassins, and he couldn't help but wonder if this Elroy guy had anything to do with that. Ulric had told Sky the Beasts had been behind that, but maybe there was more to it. Maybe Elroy and the Beasts worked together, and that wasn't good news.

Sky continued to tap his fingertips on the table until Gavin was done. Every so often, he made sure to spark a little, just to keep Gavin on task. Gavin didn't say anything, though. He didn't tell Sky he couldn't hurt him because the council needed him, and he didn't beg for his life. That was just as well. Sky couldn't hurt Gavin because he didn't have it in him, but Gavin didn't need to know that.

When Sky left the room, he was holding the list of names Gavin had given him. He handed it off to Win, who limped out of the small room without saying a word. Ulric stayed, and opened his arms. Sky didn't hesitate—he wrapped himself around his mate and rested his head against Ulric's chest.

"You were brave in there."

Sky snorted. "I didn't do anything."

"Maybe not, but you faced the man even after what he did to you. That took courage."

Sky wasn't sure of that. He couldn't look away from the window and Gavin White.

Sky wouldn't be here right now without that man. He'd still be at home, with his family, and he'd be human. He wouldn't have Ulric. He wouldn't have the assassins, who were fast becoming a family, as much as Sky's parents and siblings were.

No matter how hard dealing with his new ability had been and still was, no matter that Sky wasn't entirely human anymore, he couldn't regret what had been done to him. He hated those memories, and sometimes, he wished it had never happened, but then he looked at Ulric and Ulric looked at him, and he remembered.

The lab and his ability had given him his new life, and he wouldn't change it for anything in the world, not even getting his old life back.

You May Also Enjoy the Following from eXtasy Books Inc:

Like Storms
Catherine Lievens

Excerpt

Thor expected the text that made his phone ping to be from Tryg. He was the only person who texted Thor these days, although he'd gotten a tentative message from Isaac after Tryg had bought him a phone.

But this text wasn't from either of them. It was a blocked number, so Thor's hackles rose, but he checked it anyway. He needed to know who had his number and where they'd gotten it—and more importantly, *why* they'd looked for it.

Heard you were looking for a mage?

Thor frowned. He *was* looking for a mage, and he hadn't made a secret of it. Still, he didn't like this. *I am.* He stared at the three bouncing dots and waited for an answer.

You're in luck, then.

Am I?

Considering I'm a mage, yeah.

That was good, better than what Thor had expected. He had no idea how the mage had found his number, since Thor had limited himself to emailing the guy at the address he'd been given, but he'd find out soon enough.

How did you get my number? he asked.

Did a little digging. I had to make sure you were okay to contact. You wouldn't believe how many people want to become immortal.

Thor could easily imagine that. He'd seen the worst of what people could be and do in his long life. *I don't. I already am immortal.*

Draugr, yeah. I know. It's one of the reasons I want to meet with you and your . . . friend.

Thor's lips quirked. He wasn't sure why the emphasis on the word friend, but he wanted to find out. *When and where?*

I'm in Europe right now.

We can be there tomorrow. The cost wouldn't be a problem. He, Tryg, and Isaac could be on the next flight out, although it depended on where in Europe they needed to go and whether they decided they wanted to travel together.

Give me a few days. I'll need to travel, too.

So the mage wasn't going to meet them in his home — or in her home. Thor had no idea who he was talking with, but the person was smart. They knew better than to give out their address. *No problem. Just let me know where and when, and we'll be there.*

Good. Brussels. Three days from now.

Thor blinked. Brussels felt like a random city, although that might be because he'd never been there. Maybe not choosing a busier city like Paris or London was a good thing, or maybe this mage just liked mussels. *Like I said, we'll be there,* he answered.

What do you look like?

Thor cocked his head. This wasn't going the way he'd expected. *Why do you want to know?*

So I know who to look for.

No red roses?

Ah, no. I bet you're blond, though.

How do you know?

Draugr, remember?

Thor barked out a laugh. He didn't know what this mage

looked like, but he liked them. *I remember, trust me. And yes, I'm blond. Short hair, gray eyes, lip piercing, a few tats.*

Tall?

Yeah.

Do you look even remotely like the guy in the movie?

Thor grinned and leaned back in his office chair, propping his feet on his desk. *Why does everyone always ask that?*

Between being a draugr, blond, and being named Thor, I'm not sure why you're surprised.

True. Thor had had more than one person throwing themselves at him and asking him if he was related to that actor. *He's Australian. I'm not.*

You're from Scandinavia, yes?

Yeah. This would be easier if I could call you, you know?

It was a shot in the dark, even though it *would* be easier. But Thor wanted to hear this mage's voice. He wanted to know if he was talking to a man or a woman, and if they were as fun in person as they were over texts. He wanted to get to know the mage, because there was no way either he or Tryg were letting Isaac anywhere near this person without vetting them first. He doubted the mage would mind, since they seemed to have done the same thing.

Thor's phone rang in his hand. "My full name is Thorvald," he answered the blocked number.

"Not Thor, God of thunder?" a male voice asked.

"No, although Thorvald means follower of Thor."

"Close enough, I guess, especially if you're as tall and blond as you claim."

"You know my name, but I don't know yours," Thor rumbled. He didn't understand why he was this curious, and he didn't think the why mattered.

There was a pause, then the mage said, "Cecil."

It was an unusual name, but then, who was *Thorvald* to judge. "Nice to meet you, Cecil."

"I know you're not the one who wants to become immortal, so who is it? Why aren't they the ones talking with me?"

"Right to the point, I see."

"I have to be. I need to make sure I can trust you and your friend before I agree to meet."

"You already agreed to meet us."

"And I can as easily stay home and send you on a wild goose chase."

Thor *definitely* liked this guy. "I have a best friend."

"And you want him to be immortal."

Thor's smile widened. "Can I talk? Because it'll be faster if I do."

"I'm zipping my mouth shut."

"Right. As I was saying, I have a best friend. He's also a draugr, and he recently met a human he fell in love with." Thor didn't explain how Isaac and Tryg had met or what had happened. Cecil didn't need to know that.

"And he wants the human to become immortal."

Thor rolled his eyes. "He does. Isaac . . . he hasn't had an easy life, at all. He's happy with Tryg, and they both expected it would take years, possibly more, to find someone who could help with the mortality, which is why they've already started looking. I was lucky to find someone who knew some-one who gave me your email address, I guess."

"What's in this for you? I can meet with your friend and his boyfriend, no problem. I can't promise I'll say yes, because that will depend on how I feel about them, but I don't under-stand what you have to do with this, though."

Thor had expected the question. "Tryg and I have been friends for hundreds of years. I want him to be happy, and that will only happen if he has Isaac with him for as long as he can. I don't want him to have to watch another love die, not when there might be a way to avoid it. He'd do the same for me, and since research is what I do, I don't mind taking care of this while he takes care of Isaac."

Cecil hummed. "I see. You sound like a good man."

"I like to think I am."

"Even though you're the handler for a group of

professional killers."

Thor wasn't surprised Cecil knew. He'd done his homework, that was for sure. "I can't say that all the people I've ever worked with are good people, but I do try to make sure they only accept jobs that are warranted. Human traffickers, drug dealers, you get the idea. Many people want them dead to take their place, or to gain something from their death, or even because it's the only way they will ever pay." He hoped Cecil understood that sometimes, human justice couldn't do anything to help with that, and that those monsters needed to pay. He didn't know where Cecil's magic came from, though, so he might be a human who hadn't seen how harsh the world and the people who inhabited it could be.

Cecil cleared his throat. "Brussels, three days from now."

Thor didn't let the change of topic surprise him. "Where and when exactly?"

"I'll text you." Cecil hung up.

Thor blinked, but he didn't have time to waste. He quickly dialed Tryg's number even as he rose from his chair and headed toward his bedroom to pack.

"Thor?" Tryg asked when he answered.

"You and Isaac need to get a move on."

"You found someone?"

"Yeah. He's agreed to meet us in Brussels in three days."

"We're coming to New York. We can travel together from there."

"I'll be waiting for you."

ABOUT THE AUTHOR

Catherine lives in Italy, country of good food and hot men. She used to write fantasy as a child, but it was reading her first gay erotic romance novel that made her realize that that was what she really wanted to write.

After graduating from college in English language and translation, she divides her day between writing, reading, taking care of her son and reading some more.

You can find her on Facebook and Twitter or on her website: authorcatherinelievens.wordpress.com

Email: lievens.catherine@gmail.com

Newsletter: http://eepurl.com/c-uvKn

www.ingramcontent.com/pod-product-compliance
Lightning Source LLC
Chambersburg PA
CBHW060631130626
46555CB00002B/749